LOW OVERHEADS

Margaret Mulvihill was born and brought up in Ireland. She studied history at University College, Dublin and at Birkbeck College in London, and has worked mainly as a history editor and writer. She lives in London with a film-maker and their daughter. Her first novel, *Natural Selection*, was also published by Pandora.

LOW
OVERHEADS

**Margaret
Mulvihill**

London

First published in 1987 by
Pandora Press
(Routledge & Kegan Paul Ltd)
11 New Fetter Lane, London EC4P 4EE

Set in Sabon 10½/12 pt.
by Falcon Graphic Art Ltd
Wallington, Surrey
and printed in Great Britain
by The Guernsey Press Co Ltd
Guernsey, Channel Islands

British Library Cataloguing in Publication Data

Mulvihill, Margaret
    Low overheads.
    I. Title
    823'.914[F]   PR6063.U466

    ISBN 0–86358–139–0 (c)
          0–86358–140–4 (p)

For Conor, Brendan and Niall

CHAPTER ONE

People make their own history, though not in conditions of their own choosing, and when it comes to exercising that self-determining potential, some people have rather more choice than others. Although the historical grid within which Deborah Lieberman operated was not comparable with that of the ninth child of a widow living near an active volcano in a war-torn underdeveloped country, she liked to see her life's project in grand historical terms.

Biology had nearly knocked Deborah off course when, at the age of nineteen, she had rushed off to a registry office with Gordon Arkworth because she was afraid she was pregnant. Fortunately, her anxiety, which had been confided to no one but the putative father, proved to be groundless. But as a result of the panic marriage a hefty, liberating dollop of Arkworth capital came the student couple's way. This enabled Deborah and Gordon to spend some years abroad after graduation, mainly in Papua New Guinea. There they engaged in anthropological fieldwork as that happy-sounding combination, the husband and wife team. On their return to London a further instalment of Arkworth money facilitated the purchase of an expensive house in a cheap area. They co-authored a book about their tribe and embarked on careers that gradually diverged. Gordon Arkworth became a dealer in Pacific art objects and Deborah Lieberman established herself as an entrepreneurial guru on alternative obstetric practices.

Within a year of their homecoming, however, the Lieberman-Arkworths realized, more or less at the same

1

time, that they were conclusively bored with one another. After a series of adventures with other men and women they drifted into what was mainly, though in Deborah's case still usefully, an economic partnership. By 1979 Gordon had acquired for himself a separate flat, although he continued to use the attic of the conjugal home as a storeroom for artefacts due for restoration.

Formally, Deborah and Gordon remained friendly. The question of a divorce did not arise and they both had occasion to raise cudgels on behalf of that first joint book. So when Deborah really became pregnant she found it convenient to select her lawfully wedded husband from among the candidates available to her as the child's father. This pregnancy was not a disaster for Deborah because a baby had always been on her elastic agenda and it was the amenable Gordon's hope that an official grandchild would have a stabilizing effect upon his mother. Upon her widowhood Mrs Gloria Arkworth had encrusted her far from venerable self in the basement flat of the London house on Chapel Grove. Her establishment there was a condition for Deborah's more or less exclusive occupancy of the rest of the house.

Many were the well-wishers who secretly hoped that Deborah Lieberman would end up in hospital with a breech baby and a Caesarean section. But the body did not betray the mind and, apart from a bad dose of post-natal piles, Deborah had an easy labour in her own home and a healthy baby boy. For her son's delivery she enjoyed the facilities she made available to other expectant mothers through her business, Nativities Ltd. This was London's first 'all in' home birth agency and by the time of Orlando Lieberman's conception it was a modestly profitable concern, keeping busy two radical midwives, several obstetric and gynaecological consultants, one acupuncturist, one herbalist, a host of masseuses and a part-time astrologer. And when Deborah's younger sister Vivien finally abandoned her PhD on Coptic art, she directed some of her energy into the decoration of clients' birth rooms and the videoing of their birth throes.

But after Orlando's birth Deborah was reluctant to retire from her mission in the world. Those close to her said that her fairly immediate re-immersal in Nativities' affairs was a lucky thing because it allowed the nanny of any busy mother's dream to emerge from a quite unexpected source. About once a month or so Gordon Arkworth felt obliged to follow in his delinquent mother's footsteps, paying instead of collecting protection money against her depredations as a virtuoso shoplifter. These were not as inconvenient, financially, as they might have been because Gloria Arkworth only made off with what she could secrete in a favourite black patent leather handbag. Moreover, she did not like supermarkets and by day she seldom ventured into the West End, so Gordon's filial round was a very local one. The haberdasher's would be paid for reels of cotton, the greengrocer's for a mango, and Ahmed the newsagent for such sundries as bars of chocolate and reels of sticky tape. Mrs Arkworth had what amounted to an account at Ahmed's shop, her favourite hunting ground, and though its proprietor welcomed the business she brought, Gordon still took particular care to be on good terms with him. It chanced that, as he was writing out Ahmed's cheque, he caught sight of a neatly written notice on the counter: DAYTIME CHILDCARE AND LIGHT HOUSEHOLD DUTIES DONE FOR REASONABLE RATES. APPLY WITHIN.

'A nice quiet young lady,' Ahmed volunteered when he saw Gordon reading this card, which was destined for the shop's window. 'I told her to put the "apply within".'

'Ahem, yes,' said Gordon, aware that 'light household duties' could have many interpretations alongside advertisements for 'strict French lessons' and 'Swedish driving instruction'. To humour Ahmed Gordon told him that it might be worth the young lady's while contacting Chapel Grove about work. The household already had a cleaning

3

lady, but she did not like the basement aspect of the job because old Mrs Arkworth's habits were very private to say the least. Ahmed beamed as he restacked his newspapers. He liked to feel involved with his customers and the big houses on Chapel Grove were full of good customers.

Getting a job has so much to do with being in the right place at the right time and when Miss Cora Mangan rang the Arkworth-Lieberman doorbell a harassed Gordon was alone in the kitchen with baby Orlando. Since his sighting of the advertisement on Ahmed's counter the situation at Chapel Grove had changed to the advantage of casual seekers of employment such as Cora Mangan. When Deborah was out and the baby did not go with her, Gordon's presence in the house had become mandatory. He was the buffer against old Mrs Arkworth, whose granny mode was more hazardous than anyone could have contemplated. She ventured up from her basement flat to tickle Orlando with her plectrum nails and just a few days' previously she had been caught trying to feed him a pickled onion.

The pickled onion scandal gave the search for a nanny a new urgency but so far Deborah had only reported telephone conversations with an alarming number of listless young women from places north of Watford. Privately, Gordon blamed the wording of the nanny advertisement, feeling that Deborah's insistence on the phrase 'quiet house' put people off. He was exhausted both by the intensified monitoring of his mother's doings and by his incidental responsibility for a baby who, quite frankly, bored and disgusted him. So Gordon Arkworth welcomed Cora Mangan over the threshold and into the kitchen because a quick look over her had persuaded him to take the initiative and put her on the nanny candidate list.

Although she wasn't plain, she wasn't sexy either and that was something Deborah's friends had told her to worry about. Cora Mangan's lean but well-fed look suggested healthy eating habits. She said with an enthusiasm

4

that would have aroused suspicion in anyone but a demoralized Gordon Arkworth that she had 'loads of experience' of small babies, that she would be happy to live in and that it was her intention to study for an 'A'-level in the evenings. Now that part of her really appealed to Gordon who, though no setter of good examples himself, was a great believer in self-improvement. Cora Mangan's initial reaction to little Orlando was also encouraging. Gordon handed him over while he made coffee and was impressed when, like the Spartan boy who allowed the fox to gnaw his chest, she made no protest as Orlando's nappy, inexpertly applied by Gordon some twenty minutes earlier, came apart on her lap.

Now given the ever-worsening unemployment situation, Deborah Lieberman was in a buyers' market as far as nannies were concerned. Had Gordon quizzed Cora Mangan more exactingly he might have found out that her experience of actual babies was decidedly historic, certainly pre-disposable nappy. He could have persevered and found Deborah a trained nursery nurse with a tested vocation for this kind of work, but he was desperate and, like many unemotional people, he could be sentimental. Weren't the Irish supposed to be good with children? They had so many of them after all. Gordon voted for Cora and immediately phoned Deborah up at her clinic. She only met with serious candidates for the nanny job, and besides Cora there had been two others. (The first had been disqualified when Deborah found out that she had a boyfriend living in Germany who could only be phoned on peak rates, the second when it was discovered that her father was a butcher.)

Until Deborah arrived Orlando lay on Cora's lap and stared up in fascination at her dangly mother-of-pearl earrings. Cora twiddled his toes and suppressed her astonishment as her future employer's husband carefully removed the papers and cartons protruding from the kitchen bin, only to fold them neatly and replace them. Gordon

Arkworth was obsessively neat – his marriage had evaporated on account of incompatible table manners as much as anything else – and he could not visit his wife's household without interfering with things that upset his sense of order.

Deborah Lieberman charged into the kitchen, scooped Orlando up and, when her attention was drawn to Cora's sodden knees, remarked unapologetically that they were a nanny's occupational hazard.

'Of course,' she boomed after a pointed glance at the compressed kitchen bin, 'we women can handle the organic aspects of childcare because we're used to dealing with our own messy bodies. If you've washed your own blood-stained knickers you can handle a baby's bum.'

'Yes,' said Cora, and she answered the following barrage of questions in the same small, uncertain voice. When she faltered she was helped out by Gordon, who offered Deborah subtly edited résumés of her qualifications and conditions. But when it came to the welfare of her firstborn Deborah Lieberman was no soft touch.

'Have you asked her if she smokes?' she demanded of her husband as she thrust the classified section of a magazine under Cora's nose, 'or do you know if she's happy to be vegetarian in this house?'

'No, I don't smoke,' said Cora. But she plucked nervously at the sleeve of the sweater she'd borrowed from her smoker brother while she read the advertisement requesting a 'non-sexist, non-smoking nanny to care for Orlando in a quiet house'. 'And I've never been a great meat-eater.'

'Good. Now tell me more about yourself, about your own family? What do your parents feel about this sort of job?'

'I don't have any parents.' It was hard for Cora to avoid making this dramatic statement, 'They both died when I was little.'

Gordon practically had tears in his eyes at this revelation, but Deborah was undaunted. 'So how do you come to have the experience my husband tells me you have of looking after babies?'

'Cousins. I've got lots of young cousins and I always stayed with my aunts during school holidays.'

Deborah had stopped pacing up and down the kitchen, but Cora's ordeal was not yet over. Having consigned a repackaged and sleeping Orlando to a deckchair-like cradle, she resumed her interrogation. 'Where exactly did you say you're from?'

'Munster, southern Ireland, Munster . . . .'

'That's a bit vague isn't it? We might as well say we live in the western hemisphere.' Despite her sarcasm Deborah's voice had softened, probably because she was afraid of waking Orlando up.

'Rathbwee,' Cora had to mumble and then, as she'd dreaded, Gordon looked at her with renewed interest.

'Where that IRA siege was?' When Cora nodded he turned to Deborah. 'You *must* remember? Where they caught up with that fat terrorist Frank wrote about. What was his name?'

But Cora looked blank and said she hadn't been at home when the siege happened. Luckily for her nerve, Deborah refused to take any interest. She may have seen Gordon's interest as a diversion and did not react when he tittered suddenly and said, 'Raging Bull Riordan. What a name!'

The rest of Cora's 'interview' took place between Gordon and Deborah. Cora sat down with her cup of coffee and listened, nodding at either one of them every now and then, and generally behaving as though she were a judge presiding over a court rather than the person in the dock.

She could tell certain things about her employers just from their appearances. For a start, it was obvious that the Arkworth-Lieberman romance had not been a narcissistic one. Here were no Mick and Bianca. Gordon had a scrubbed confection of a face, with glazed pinkish skin and a meringue of blond hair perched far back on his skull. He spoke quickly and fastidiously, his lips moving as though

7

they were being manipulated by a puppeteer, and he almost shuddered when Deborah offered him a slice of crumbly fruit cake to go with his coffee.

What a contrast the monumental Deborah presented. She was intimidatingly fat and her clothes hung round her in a robe-like way. Her fingers were covered by big Borgia-poisoner rings and a string of amber beads hung around her neck like a chain of office. Cora eyed the debating pair in the same shifty way that as a child she had examined the hairy mole on the chin of one of her aunts. How, she wondered, had they produced Orlando? It was too early to say which way he would go, and both of his parents had blue eyes, but a physical compromise was unthinkable.

As Deborah orated on, and bits of her fruit cake cascaded to the floor, Gordon began to look irritated. Finally, to his obvious relief, she swung around to ask Cora how soon she could start.

'Next week if you like?' Cora could have said 'right now' but she was smart enough to know that it would sound better if she were not quite so available as that.

Gordon looked imploringly at Deborah. He was as anxious as she was to reinstate the amiable distance that normally lay between them. Apart from his business, which took him abroad for much of the year, his involvement with Orlando plucked at his conscience, for he did feel a responsibility for the son born to one of his regular lovers who was now out of nappies and therefore more appealing. As for Deborah, she wanted Gordon the bin-tamer out of her house as soon as possible. At the same time there was an urgent need of someone to dilute the dangerous proximity of her mother-in-law. So it was all settled there and then. Cora's trial period would begin on the following Sunday afternoon, when she could observe Orlando's routines and have her first supper at Chapel Grove.

*

8

The appointed Sunday came and Cora, rucksack on her back, set off like Dick Whittington to make her fortune. Deborah led her to the room next to Orlando's nursery on the first floor. She was brisk but more friendly than she'd been at the interview, offering an apology for the books still lining the room's walls, which Cora said she didn't mind, and promising her a television of her own within a couple of weeks. Cora was then left to unpack. This process took an unseemly five minutes and so, having hoisted her deflated rucksack to the top of the wardrobe, she spent another half hour marvelling at a room in which you could have swung a tiger.

Napoleon's army marched no faster than Julius Caesar's and Cora Mangan's journey to England was no different from that undertaken by her illiterate great grand-aunts. It was less than two months since that cold, black night in November when she'd crept into North Wales, past the misty Telford Bridge and down to London through the grimy heart of old industrial England. Through half-closed eyes she'd peeped at the other women passengers with their mouths sewn as thin lines on their weary faces and their swollen feet squashed into cheap shoes. Something like aversion therapy had made her come to the assistance of one such luggage-laden mother of two, for whom she had battled her way through anorak-strewn bodies and standing men to bring back cupfuls of sweet strong tea and platefuls of overpriced chips. This woman's baby son had been about the same age as Orlando was when Cora first took charge of him. Every time the boat-baby had spat out his blue plastic dummy, his mother had reverently sucked it clean and plugged him up again.

But little Orlando had nothing blue. His clothes were made of natural fibres and he slept on a lambskin fleece. There was no washable wallpaper in the house on Chapel Grove and food had to be decanted into heavy ceramic jars. Had it not been for some pragmatic compromises, such as the provision of disposable nappies, Cora might

9

have found intolerable her employer's feelings for what she called the 'physicality of life'. But for all its Bohemian squalor, the house had a reassuringly moneyed air, and there was no stinting on hot water or central heating. The great kitchen, which took up most of the ground floor, was a wonderfully warm and welcoming place, the lingering sweetness of the still-life mounds of fruit matched by the comforting smell of damp washing. Like a medieval hall, the kitchen was the site of all household comings and goings, all cooking and meal-taking. Cora was happy to spend most of her time there, especially since it housed the apparatus that freed her physically from the baby. While Orlando cooed at her from his bouncer, she learned how to use the range and she was soon skilled at chopping vegetables on the huge wooden table.

Cora found shelter within this house and in time she got used to Deborah's rhetorical modes of address. For a girl whose head still reverberated with Aunty Bernie's insistence that her flat feet precluded a career in nursing, Aunty Liz's pessimism about her height and her French for Aer Lingus, and the head nun's doleful deliberations on her lack of 'drive', Chapel Grove offered a good halfway house towards something less depressingly grounded in her physique and her immediate personality. It would, she hoped, make up for a first false start in adult life.

Within a matter of weeks Deborah came to think highly of her husband's impulsive presentation of Cora, even though she had come without any references and had never heard of sexism. Deborah had been put off the idea of a truly foreign au pair by tales of gigantic phone bills and unruly lovers, but quiet Cora seemed without any expensive or disruptive habits. She had been pointedly supplied with a double bed but she had no followers of that kind, and her brother appeared to be her only connection with the world outside Chapel Grove. Better still, this sparse social life did not mean that Cora 'hung around' when

Deborah wanted to believe that she was alone in her own home with her baby or entertaining her friends. No, Cora was happy to stay in her room and study, and at the same time she was nearly always available for extra babysitting. Deborah lost no time in coming to a verbal agreement with her that she should stay for a year and then, all continuing well, negotiate a further term of office.

The only spanner in the works was Mrs Gloria Arkworth, who did not at first take to Deborah's nanny. The old lady's appearance had startled Cora, for the chainsmoking begetter of Gordon was no Mother Hubbard. She always wore the same clothes – black stretch ski pants topped by a black and gold polo-neck sweater – which Cora charitably assumed to be duplicated. When outdoors this outfit was completed by a mock leopardskin jacket and a black chiffon scarf, so that from behind Gloria Arkworth looked decades younger than the seventy-odd she allegedly was. Indeed, Mrs Arkworth scuttled down the high street as though she still hoped to find, moored outside the dry cleaner's, the yacht of some fabulously hedonistic plutocrat.

Not unreasonably, Mrs Arkworth perceived Cora as a spy on her own doings. She covered herself by waylaying Deborah in Cora's first weeks to tell her that the nanny, a 'regular sloppy-knickers', had men hidden all over the house. But these accusations were taken by Deborah as a heartening indication of her nanny's proper loyalties, because on most other occasions Gloria made no secret of her loathing of her daughter-in-law (a loathing Deborah had elevated into anti-Semitism). Deborah told Cora not to be upset by Mrs Arkworth's rantings and Cora did not dare tell her that they might have had their basis in her brother's visits to the house. For if he were coming from a dirty job, Patrick Mangan often took advantage of Chapel Grove's luxurious sanitary facilities.

CHAPTER TWO

It was Vivien Lieberman's predicament to be the charismatic Deborah's little sister. Vivien tried to keep out of her big sister's shade by emphasizing their differences, both physical and psychological. It helped that she was as slender as Deborah was fat, and she downplayed her equally extended education by speaking with a mock proletarian drawl. Whereas Deborah was Jungian in sympathy, Vivien professed to prefer Freud, vinaigrette to mayonnaise, and so on. Deborah Lieberman was a religiously thorough consumer, buying nothing for her baby that could not withstand an extraordinary range of unlikely hazards, while Vivien was thrillingly extravagant. But Vivien hadn't found herself a rich ex-husband and so she had to maintain the lifestyle she had accustomed herself to through an inglorious combination of begging from her stepfather, miscellaneous freelancing for her sister and the most casual teaching jobs.

The outer rooms of Deborah's business headquarters were empty when Vivien arrived one morning in search of a cheque for her work on Nativities' latest mail order catalogue. An 'in session' notice was pinned to the Experience Room's door, through which a soft American voice seeped. This was the sound of one Lincoln Baker, the self-styled transpersonal therapist imported in connection with Nativities' latest scheme. Deborah was playing with the idea of reviving the couvade, a custom described by anthropologists and historians whereby fathers participate in the mysteries of the birth process by mimicking pregnancy and sharing in the accouchement period. If war were a product of male menstruation envy, Deborah reasoned, what were the consequences of birth envy?

Vivien moved away from the droning, incantatory voice of Lincoln Baker and took advantage of her sister's preoccupation to search through various out-trays for that cheque. But ten minutes of discreet rifling gave her no joy. Instead, the draft of a letter to clients on the couvade venture, which was lying on Deborah's desk, caught her attention.

'Since 1976 Nativities has been offering women an unrivalled care and celebration service for the birthdays of their children. Over the years we pride ourselves on having offered our clients all that they have required to make the immediate experience of motherhood a joyous one. We believe that fathers, too, would testify to the value of our role, both for the comfort of their partners, and their babies, and for their own satisfaction at a time, perhaps the only time, when they can only bear witness. It is because of this very factor that Nativities is now proposing to expand its programme to specifically accommodate fathers via a couvade course, which may soon establish itself as an integral element in a Nativities' birth . . . .'

Here the letter trailed off and marks in the margin – 'will they understand this?', 'too academic' – signalled its author's dissatisfactions. Vivien was sniggering over a reread when the telephone began to ring. As the answering machine clicked into action a flushed Deborah tiptoed into the room.

'Vivien! How nice of you to come. It's all going wonderfully. You really must come and see what they're up to.' Deborah plucked Vivien's arm out of the filing cabinet containing the petty cash box and led her to the spyhole positioned on the Experience Room door. Vivien obliged by peering into its candlelit interior. Most of the Nativities staffers were sitting on cushions around the perimeter of the room and in its centre seven men, with Lincoln presiding offside, were locked into a phalanx-like formation and breathing heavily.

'It's a rugby scrum?' Vivien turned round on her sister, who responded with an excited whisper, 'Yes, that's it. We've had a marvellous discussion when they talked about important physical experiences and Lincoln came up with this. It's like giving birth, you see, getting the ball out. The same kind of controlled violence.'

Vivien looked in again. Now the men were rotating slowly, with hands pushed into their neighbour's shoulder, and all the while Lincoln droned on about helping the ball to be born. But then Vivien shrank back as though someone had poked her in the eye through the spyhole. There was no mistaking the rear-end of one of Deborah's couvade guinea pigs, for among that scrummage was definitely one, and God knew how many more, of her own ex-lovers. But Vivien didn't risk mentioning this to Deborah because they had already had several rows about her habit of remaining on excellent terms with the men she'd finished with. She just said,

'Actually, I've got to split now. I'm meeting Leonie Baxter for lunch. Remember? I just thought you might have my money.'

'But we're all going to have some tea in a few minutes,' Deborah sounded offended, 'and it would be a chance for you to meet Lincoln properly. He's really very sweet you know. . . .'

'Ta very much, but I wouldn't like to spoil my appetite, and I don't suppose we'll get much of a chance to talk about what I'm supposed to tell Leonie?'

Deborah's face had gone all vague and mystical again at the mention of Vivien's cheque but the name Leonie Baxter forced pound signs into her eyes. 'Just talk naturally to her,' she said with something nearer her normal volume, 'only make sure that we see whatever she writes before anything gets printed. She'll have to interview me eventually as well.' Then, in strategic consideration of the import-

14

ance of her sister's loyalty, Deborah allowed Vivien to dip into the petty cash box. And before there was any danger of encountering the long-arsed Greg whose squash racquet was still in her hall cupboard, Vivien sloped off to her lunch date.

Leonie Baxter made a good living for herself telling much of the English-speaking world about how she coped with the outrageous slings and arrows of her daily life: the vagaries of maintenance men; the male chauvinist thuggery of dustbin-men, the tribulations of various nieces in inner-city schools, dog shit in her patio, parking at Heath-row, etcetera. Vivien, whose real identity was always cloaked by a lazy pseudonym – Vicky Lehman, Valerie Levine – had provided Leonie with material on several occasions: once for an article about 'revolting women', another time for a piece about cystitis-sufferers. Most recently, Vivien had fleshed out what Leonie called one of her hardy annuals, an extended deliberation on the *anomie* of heterosexual women in search of compatible men in cities such as London, New York and Sydney. This was a subject to which, as a discreet and rather above-it-all lesbian, Leonie could bring the same compassion that she brought to the plight of disabled people looking for economical cars.

But on this occasion Vivien's real identity was not going to be a problem because Leonie wished to write a series of articles about real-life sisters, to see just how 'sisterly' they were in the wider sense of that word. Deborah had encouraged Vivien to cooperate because she thought that Leonie with her media contacts should be kept well-oiled.

So loyal Vivien sat with glazed eyes in a Soho restaurant until Leonie arrived, breathless and clutching a cab receipt. Having knocked Vivien sideways with a killer suede satchel, she pushed her into the cheaper brasserie section of the restaurant, plonked a tiny cassette recorder on their table and ordered two glasses of dry white wine. Routine

15

enquiries about each other's welfare were then exchanged, Leonie telling Vivien about the unfortunate last-minute cancellation of a holiday due to her partner's responsibilities as a mother.

'That's a shame,' Vivien volunteered, rather woodenly. She was thinking cattily that Leonie showed her age by looking so youthful. She maintained her very blonde curls and a permanent tan almost as if she were being paid by the Arts Council to do so. That wasn't such a spiteful idea because Leonie had experienced alternative medicine, even double glazing, at the expense of people who had hoped that she would write about their services. But though Vivien was not in a charitable mood she was extremely hungry. Her mouth was fiery with the unexpected whole peppercorns lodged in her pâté when Leonie began to speak her preliminaries into the recording machine.

'When Deborah Lieberman started up Nativities she was operating from her own home and her sister Vivien got involved by helping her with publicity. . . .'

'Yes and no,' Vivien choked out, and Leonie looked at her expectantly. 'I mean Debbo didn't ever start up in that sense. She was running a sort of informal advice thing for women who wanted to have their babies at home. It was just after her book had come out and it got round the grapevine that she was a good person to invite to a birth. You know, like some people get invited to every party. But it wasn't a business or anything like that. It didn't have a name or anything. In fact, the name was my idea.'

'I never knew that.'

Leonie's feigned surprise was mollifying. With a certain pride in her voice Vivien continued, 'Yeah. I was still doing my thesis then, so I thought up the name Nativities and found the picture of Isis with Horus that's on all the notepaper and stuff.'

'But haven't you been involved in other ways?'

'Not really. It's Debbo's thing. I just help sometimes.'

'Didn't it ever feel odd being involved with something

16

you hadn't any experience of, not being a mother your-self?'

'Neither had Deborah then. What's this got to do with our sisterliness anyhow?'

'Sorry,' Leonie switched off her machine, 'just a digres-sion.'

'Yeah.' Vivien was now fretting about her main course. But since the recording machine was off she forgot the professional nature of the encounter enough to say, 'You know I've never had Debbo's chutzpah. Most of her early clients were mates and she didn't start charging anything until the thing got so big she had to get proper premises and staff.'

Leonie then tried without success to get her machine going again, so she abandoned it and took a spiral-bound notebook from her satchel. She continued the conversation by asking Vivien how her latest project was going. Vivien's schemes were always projects, never products, and so this enquiry was a slightly sadistic one because Leonie was in no need of a consolatory reminder of the failures of her old schoolfriends.

'I'm having to restructure it,' Vivien said, looking away from her. She was understandably reluctant to tell Leonie about the rejection letter she'd received that very morning from the most likely publisher of a book about the iconographic history of the special relationship between women and cats. She ignored Leonie's suggestion that she should turn her synopsis into an article and, head down, enthusiastically tackled one of the walnut and mussel salads that had finally arrived at their table. Soon, how-ever, Leonie began again.

'Now I'd like to get more from you about what it's like to be sisters working together in the context of the women's movement.'

'It's not like that. I'm not as involved as you think. . . .'

'Come on Viv,' Leonie wagged a diamond-studded little finger, 'what's big sister like as the boss?'

17

'For fuck's sake, don't call Deborah big. She's very sensitive about that. Of course she's always been older and bigger than me, but Nativities is her baby not mine.'

'But she does have a real baby now.'

'Yeah,' Vivien laid down her fork and lapsed into a distant fondness, 'she's mad about him.'

'If you had a baby yourself, would you want Deborah at the birth?'

Vivien laughed bleakly and said wearily, 'I don't think that's likely. I reckon I'm like a lay sister, you know, the ones who don't take all the vows.'

'Oh I like that,' Leonie wiped her lips and seized her notebook, 'a lay sister. Why don't you want to join the mothers' army?'

'Maybe I do really. I don't know. It's just that I'm a bit suspicious of it all. I mean a lot of Debbo's clients are into the organic trip, big tits and cuddly babies, but nobody thinks about mothering stroppy adolescents do they?'

'Too right,' was Leonie's vehement response, 'and that's exactly what I've got via Marlene. She lets the brat get away with murder. Honestly, last weekend. . . .' Leonie stopped suddenly and frowningly plucked a hair from her salad. She summoned the waitress and began an irate discourse with her although, as a futuristic redhead, she was hardly responsible for the blonde hair defiling Leonie's salad. But the upshot of this argument was that both salads were confiscated and so, after noting with some dismay that the ashtray had been emptied of what had been by her standards a perfectly re-lightable butt, Vivien lit a cigarette.

Vivien was in solidarity with the waitress. If she had found a hair in her salad she might at first have wondered if it were one of her own, just as her reaction to bad breath was usually an enquiry into her own state. With the radiant Leonie Vivien felt burdened by such lingering principles. She hadn't married her supervisor and one way or another that had cost her the completion of her doctorate. She still

18

refused to buy fruit from South Africa, Chile or Israel and she bought expensive Nicaraguan coffee. When the salads were re-presented she smiled at the waitress, who nonetheless got her revenge by staying down the other end of the dining room when it was time to consider a dessert. When the waitress did come near their table again Leonie decided that there was only time for coffee, and then the coffee-taking was interrupted by the people who kept coming up to Leonie to ask her how she was, how Marlene was, whether she'd read so and so's book or been to so and so's preview. Vivien looked so worn down that Leonie didn't even bother to introduce her.

'I can't promise anything,' she said as they waited in the street outside for a vacant taxi, 'and I'll have to see Deborah too, but I should get something together quite quickly.'

'We'll have to see what you write though.' Vivien couldn't be sure that Leonie heard her above the noise of the taxi's engine. She just yelled out before slamming the door, 'They'll ring you to arrange a photo session.'

As Vivien stood in the street it started to rain, so heavily and suddenly that it was like a theatrical deluge, and that suited her mood perfectly. She licked the drops that fell on her face with a melodramatic satisfaction and when bullets of water began to bounce on the pavement around her she did not rush for shelter.

The rain seemed to have come down in solidarity with her, having all the dimensions of her anger and disappointment. In fact it seemed to Vivien that shit had been raining on her life for the previous eighteen months and she didn't see the point of seeking shelter any longer. By enduring the deluge there was a chance it might stop as suddenly as it had begun.

In spite of looks, brains and friends Vivien Lieberman was as miserable as sin. She worried in case she'd made Leonie Baxter aware of her resentment of an older sister who just seemed to be devastatingly lucky. Deborah made money through an enterprise with overtones of political credibility and she had a baby and security of status without being married in any oppressive sense. She even had the nerve to insist on an uncomplicated friendship with several of Vivien's ex-lovers, men Vivien herself preferred to relegate to a rogues' gallery of the past imperfect.

Fingering the notes her sister had given her that morning, Vivien hailed the next vacant cab to turn into the street with less assurance but the same effect as Leonie. Its driver explained that traffic was being held up all over the West End on account of a bomb scare. 'Bloody Irish. If it's not them it's our colonial friends.'

Vivien bit her lip and climbed in. She wasn't going to argue with him, having no such strength left, but she didn't tip him and then, for fear of his abuse, she belted into the doorway of her flat. She was wet through and through, and once in her living room she peeled off her outer clothes, turned up the heating and began a wild dance, flailing her arms about and stamping her feet. She ignored her cat, who cruised her vicinity with an expectant purr, confident that this caper was some novel preliminary to a bonus feed. But Genghis was to be disappointed for his mistress sat on her sofa for a long time, massaging her itchy scalp with a bath towel and hypnotizing herself with the watery hush of the cars passing in the street outside.

Eventually she stomped into the kitchen to make herself some more coffee. Meanwhile Genghis rubbed his back against the fridge door, across which, in magnetic letters the slogan 'a woman without a man is like a fish without a bicycle' was emblazoned. It had been sent by a more principled friend after one of the most humiliating chapters in Vivien's disastrous emotional history. This had involved the miner she had put up in her flat during the great strike. After a few weeks of passionate lobbying of Parliament, and of his unduly supportive hostess, he had gone back to his wife in Yorkshire, leaving Vivien with an enormous

20

phone bill. Then, to cap the indignity of it all, he had turned scab and returned to work.

'But Gengi sweetheart,' Vivien said as she filled her cat's plate in token of her unabating faith in the sex he had been born into, 'I do so like bicycles.' She felt better now that she was warmer and dryer. She chucked the publisher's rejection letter into a bin instead of filing it with all the others she'd received, and decided to do the obvious thing to get hold of more money. She picked up her telephone and dialled her stepfather's apartment in Manhattan. When his answering machine began to respond, she swore and put the phone down for a moment only to pick it up again and dial his office. Again she listened to a recorded message. But her resolve had hardened now so she found the number of his country house in Maine.

'Hi,' said a neat little American voice.

'Is Sidney Weiss there?'

'No. Who is this calling?'

'It's his stepdaughter Vivien Lieberman.'

'Vivien! I'm looking forward to meeting you. Sidney has told me all about your book.'

'Oh has he?' Vivien was wincing.

'Yes.' The voice added shyly, 'I'm Sophie. I guess he's told you about us.'

He hadn't but Vivien now knew that she was speaking with the latest applicant Mrs Weiss, the last wife having been despatched after the usual two-year term of office. Vivien and Deborah's continuing status as stepdaughters of the womanizing Sidney was in no small way due to the fact that precious few other women had managed to find a permanent place in his life. If the installation of this Sophie at Maine was an indication of serious business, there was one crucial enquiry to be made. Vivien asked Sophie about the kitchen, for the first step taken by Sidney's wives, as opposed to transitional lovers, was the refurbishment of his many kitchens, there being always something unsatisfactory about their décor.

21

'Are you doing some decorating at Maine?'

'Well, just a little,' Sophie laughed. 'I just had to get rid of those awful colonial-style closets.'

Vivien bit the only decent nail left to her after a week of anxious chewing. When Sophie had finished telling her about some Dutch tiles she'd ordered, she asked if there was a message to be relayed to Sidney.

'Yes,' said a suddenly inspired Vivien, 'tell him I've decided to get married, and if he phones me soon I'll tell him about it.'

'Oooh,' Sophie crooned, 'and he might have some news for you.'

On that note of coy confidentiality Vivien finished her first conversation with her stepfather's sixth intended.

CHAPTER THREE

Patrick Mangan could not bring himself to be enthusiastic about his little sister's first job in England. He was an artisan with an Open University degree and, as with those autodidact cobbler and printer radicals of old, this went with a stroppy political conscience. The very word 'nanny' was distasteful to him, causing him to wrinkle his elegantly welded nose and to think aloud about African 'boys'. But after a few trips to Chapel Grove, usually when Deborah was out, Patrick began to mellow.

'Your guilty liberal is a great woman,' he would say as he scoffed avocado sandwiches and sat back in the best kitchen chair, where he might not have felt so comfortable had he known it was a Melanesian fertility seat. Apart from dealing with the still very local impact of Orlando's routines, and doing some cooking and shopping, Cora was no general skivvy. She was reasonably paid, considering she had full board and lodging for free, and they (rather she since hubby had retreated from the day-to-day scene) were encouraging her with the night class. There was even talk of providing Cora with driving tuition.

Patrick Mangan was still not sure if his sister was deep or dull, perhaps both, but her easy integration at Chapel Grove showed that there was such a thing as happy self-exploitation. After all, he said to himself, some black Americans may well have been better off as slaves on paternalistic plantations than they were as wage slaves in the industrial cities of the North. But Patrick's most serious and frequently articulated misgiving about the nanny job was its possibly distressing effect on a young woman recovering from the psychological aftermath of an abortion. Even on this score Cora had been reassuringly firm. She insisted that her experience with Orlando confirmed her in that decision because it provided her with an hourly reminder of the energy and the money required for a proper rearing, and she had never seen adoption as a bearable alternative.

Cora's feelings about what a baby required were probably informed by a sense of her own privations. As the orphaned poor relations of their parents' siblings she and, to a lesser extent, Patrick had had the sort of childhood that was common in Victorian times. With the help of their father's only brother Uncle Willy, Patrick had left for England when he was seventeen, and a collection of aunts took care of Cora in turn. Her Aunty Liz paid for her First Communion outfit, her Aunty Bernie for new shoes and music lessons, and her Aunty Eileen, who had no children of her own until she adopted twins when Cora was twelve, looked after almost every other expense. Patrick saw his sister at Christmas and in summer, when she usually stayed with her Uncle Willy in the Mangan ancestral township of Rathbwee. There, Patrick had taught his sister how to ride a bike and bought her a record player.

When Cora finished school a conclave of aunts discussed her future, paying about as much attention to her own wishes as Deborah and Gordon had during her 'interview'. The aunts agreed that, after a final summer in Rathbwee, she should go to Dublin and stay with her Aunty Eileen while attending a secretarial course. Uncle Willy had absented himself from these discussions because he did not feel competent to discuss a girl's future. Besides, no heed would have been paid to his thoughts, for Willy was in bad odour with his sisters-in-law: the aunts, having failed to rescue their sister from a disastrous marriage into the Mangan 'bad blood', of which Willy was a vigorous

24

reminder, were determined to protect their niece from it. Hadn't that Willy Mangan fought against Franco, been interned as an active Republican during the Emergency of the 1940s, and come back to Rathbwee to open his pub wearing drainpipe trousers?

Patrick Mangan, whose potential as a carrier of the patrilineal bad blood had yet to be assessed, had expected a qualified, marketable sister to join him in London. Instead he found her on his doorstep within a matter of months, without a certificate declaring her competence on some kind of keyboard and with a tendency to sudden nausea. First things first was his response, although he was considerate enough to offer himself as a willing uncle and not too obviously relieved when Cora herself suggested an abortion. She was well aware of that option on account of her Aunty Eileen's frenzied involvement with an organization that worried more about the unborn than living women, let alone the millions of unwanted children born into suffering. So effectively had this aunt's propaganda boomeranged on Cora that she was almost disappointed not to see women 'sleeping around' all over London, laying down their languorous heads wherever they could and now and then tossing babies into the incinerators placed at every street corner.

Cora spent her savings from her summer work in Willy's bar on the abortion and Patrick did his best to look after her. He held her hand when they returned from the clinic in Surrey in a taxi and insisted that she stayed in bed for a week. When she was less pale he took time off to take her round the sights, and he put no pressure on her to find work until he was sure she was completely recovered, physically. She never told him directly how, rather by whom, she had become pregnant, but that didn't stop Patrick from building himself a plausible picture. It seemed that it had happened after her first time and that the father was some American hippy. (Anyone who passed through Rathbwee with a backpack was a hippy.) This Yank made his living selling seashell jewellery to real tourists, hence the mother-of-pearl earrings that had so endeared Cora to Orlando.

But now things had settled down well enough. Patrick had written to Willy, and Cora had written to her Aunty Eileen, telling them both that she'd come by an extremely interesting job as an administrative assistant to a lady authoress. This job title was inspired by Deborah's strategy for making Cora's service a tax-deductible one.

Late one morning, when Orlando was playing with his toes in the kitchen and Patrick was relaxing in the magnificent bathroom on the nursery floor, Vivien Lieberman arrived unexpectedly. Hearing the commotion she caused, Patrick quickly replaced the lid on a tub of Nativities herbal back-relieving cream and reached for a soft towel. He pulled on the clean clothes he had brought with him – his work clothes were going through their weekly odyssey in the Lieberman washing machinery – and hastened down to the hall. There, Deborah's sister was swearing at the large cupboard box full of Nativities catalogues she had just heaved inside the front door.

'Fucking shit,' she said, pushing the hair back from her eyes, 'I thought Debbo'd be here to help me lug this lot in.'

She was startled by the sight of Patrick on the threshold, volunteering to help. Until Cora introduced him she thought, like the discreet matrons at the abortion referral clinic, that the Mangan siblings were lovers. They were so unalike, at least on first impression. Small and brown-haired, Cora could be fleetingly pretty but her black-haired brother was a real door-darkener of a man. He was the very picture of your romantic, rugged Celt and, as Viven later confided to her diary, the most fuckable being on two legs that she'd clapped eyes on in a year of virtual celibacy. Although she suppressed her urge to stand back and say 'Wow!' Vivien's admiration was unmistakable as she allowed Patrick to heave her box of catalogues into the kitchen.

26

When Vivien said she'd 'adore' to share some lunch with them, Cora smiled to herself because she was as proud of her brother as he was protective of her. For years she had longed for Patrick to visit her at boarding school so that she could confirm the status she enjoyed by virtue of her possession of his photograph, but he never came. Now she enjoyed watching Vivien trying to impress him. Physically, this was not hard because Vivien had a body that oppressed most women because of its conformity with a rare fantasy stereotype: thick hair around a thin face, no bum to speak of on top of long legs, and improbably large breasts. Now she pirouetted around the kitchen in fetishistic little ankle boots, one hand on her hip to draw attention to her dramatically belted waist, the other waving the cigarette accepted from Patrick. Suddenly she stopped and in an accusing voice asked Cora what kind of soup she was stirring.

'Last night's lentil.'

'Orlando's had a shit then.'

'No,' Cora was firm. She abandoned the soup and hoisted Orlando up so that she could smell his bulky rear end. 'He's just farting that's all.' When she put him back on his prayer-mat she knew that Vivien was right but had decided that she wasn't going to change him until she had her own lunch inside her. Patrick said nothing but once the table had been set he put out his cigarette and urged Cora to sit down. By then, however, Orlando's productivity was unmistakable and with a groan about his timing, Cora took him off to the nursery.

'You don't look very like your sister,' Vivien said when Cora had left the room.

'No, she's like our mother and I'm like our father.' Unlike Cora, whose speech was spattered with such items as the 'hot press' which Deborah was still learning to translate, Patrick spoke with a more neutral mid-Atlantic accent.

'We,' Vivien continued, 'I mean Debbo and me, we lost

27

our Mum about ten years ago, and I don't even remember Dad.'

'Any other family?' asked Patrick sympathetically.

'Well, sort of, sort of lateral relations if you know what I mean.'

But Patrick looked as if he didn't.

'I mean we've got a stepfather who's still quite interested in us, me anyway, because our Mum was the only one of his wives to die in harness so to speak. But he lives in the States now, and he hates flying so that doesn't really amount to much.'

Patrick nodded and then eyed the steaming soup tureen on the table. But his conscience told him he should wait for Cora before tucking in, so he rose and walked down the room to examine the sand painting hanging on the wall beside the dresser.

'Nice piece of work,' he said politely to Vivien, who had followed him.

'Yeah,' she smiled conspiratorially up at him, 'my brother-in-law sells them. He's having an exhibition soon. Maybe you'd like to come?'

Before Patrick could say anything conclusive to this invitation Cora returned with a fragrant and socially acceptable Orlando. Vivien took him on her lap while Cora ate her lunch and she enjoyed the sight of Patrick plastering butter on his bread like a gastronomic John Wayne. But before there was any danger of participation in the clearing up, Vivien decided to 'shift her ass'. As she slammed the front door behind her Patrick turned to Cora and said, 'It looks as if that one was pushed from the trough by the big sister.'

Then the clean and fed Patrick Mangan turned to a family matter. Producing a crumpled piece of lined blue notepaper from the breast pocket of his jacket he said, 'I had a letter this morning from our dear Uncle Willy, which, between its lines, might explain some odd little happenings.'

28

'Oh yes?' said Cora, deftly rescuing the spoonful of mashed banana sliding off Orlando's chin.

'Yes. What exactly did he give you to bring over?'

Cora sighed and put one hand over her mouth to signal some embarrassment. 'Willy did give me two packets to take over for you, but I lost one of them on the boat. I think it was the brown bread and white pudding, at least that's what it felt like. I was in such a state I never asked him. And you were all sarcastic about the other parcel, after just a look at it, so I didn't think you'd be missing the one I lost.'

'You never opened it?'

'No, honest to God. You know Willy's parcels. It was all done up with loads and loads of brown paper and string. And I never thought you'd be worrying about a bit of brown bread.' Cora was feeling very resentful. What was the point of bringing all this up now? Patrick gave her a solemn look and tapped the rim of his mug impatiently.

'Willy,' he said eventually, 'is a bit behind the times, a bit of a romantic, and I think that, along with Dad's gold watch, he must have taken the opportunity provided by your leaving to pass something on to the lads via me.'

'What stuff?' Cora asked, having a good idea who her patriotic uncle's lads were likely to be.

'God knows.' Patrick raised his hands in irritation. 'Money maybe, money in used English notes that fatty Riordan might have had. Willy would have been the obvious person to leave it with.'

Cora fell silent, bitterly recalling how she'd scrounged around to get the money for England and her abortion. She'd been counting out her own resources while Raging Bull Riordan's little nest-egg had been sitting on top of her rucksack. She also resented her uncle's continual presumption of a direct male line of communication. Willy hadn't bothered to tell her that she had custody of her father's gold watch, so automatically bestowed on Patrick, and he'd made such a song and dance about giving her fifty quid from the money he'd codded out of various journalists for his background information about the Siege of Rathbwee.

'Anyhow,' Patrick sought her attention again, 'there's no use in jumping to drastic conclusions about this parcel business. But I have been wondering why our local ambassador for the cause of freedom has been down in the Crown every night for the past week, asking me ever so considerately how my sister's doing for herself and giving me the cold eye when I tell him she's just fine thank you very much.'

Patrick rose from the table and looked businesslike. 'Let's have a look at that other parcel. That'll be a clue to our misdemeanour.'

But Orlando had started to cry and so before taking Patrick up to her room Cora had to walk up and down the kitchen with him, allowing him to finger the curtains with his banana-slimy fingers. When he had calmed down they all went upstairs. Orlando was propped up on the bed like a Buddha while Cora found the parcel in the bottom of her wardrobe. Patrick ripped the string around it with his penknife and emptied the shoebox beneath its many wrappings of brown paper out on to the floor.

'Well now, will you look here,' he said as he grabbed Cora's nightie and peeled the tinfoil from an old but well maintained Luger pistol. Patrick held the gun aloft and surveyed it with disdainful interest.

'This, you can be sure,' he winked at Orlando, 'this little beauty was our bold Willy's personal contribution to the struggle. It must have been hanging around since the fifties campaign.'

'What will we do?' Cora was very worried now.

'We'll just have to tell my friend the plain and unadorned truth, and he'll have to believe us. If he doesn't, I'll show him my accounts.' With that Patrick laughed and picked up Orlando, and Cora tried to take comfort in the familiar rhythm of her relationship with her brother.

Patrick had a way of being grim one moment and cheerful the next, as if he felt a need to impress upon Cora the seriousness of a situation before he could offer his brotherly reassurance.

'Pity you didn't leave that on the boat instead,' he said, kicking the shoebox, 'but put Willy's baby back in its cot for now and I'll go and find it a home in some nice skip.' Following Patrick's example, Cora held the gun with her nightie as she replaced it in the box and handed it over. 'I'll see you in the Crown on Sunday,' he said as he bounded back down the stairs.

But less than twenty minutes later Patrick was back, holding a plastic carrier bag containing a bunch of bananas and the shoebox. 'Look. I don't want to seem paranoid but I think this place is being watched, so I just went round the corner and bought the young fellah some more bananas. Don't look now mind, but hang on to the Luger for the time being. If anyone finds it, just say it's a Mangan family heirloom.'

Dutifully, Cora took the box and the bananas and then she began to dress Orlando for his afternoon round of the local park. Before she left the house she peeped outside the kitchen window. And there he was, near the guard dog's kennel in the builders' supply yard across from the house. This watcher-man was tall and he wore glasses. As he walked slowly away and down Chapel Grove he paused to cup his hands around a cigarette lighter, just like a detective in a 1940s movie.

CHAPTER FOUR

Deborah Lieberman enjoyed telling people that she woke first thing in the morning as pure matter, acquired her human essence after coffee and the crowning refinement of her femininity only when she reached her desk. But this leisurely transition had been greatly speeded up by Orlando's arrival, and so Deborah's musings adapted accordingly. Now she said that the urgency of her baby's morning schedule was a reminder of the fact that the word *materia*, Latin for matter, was derived from *mater*, or mother, from whom or which all beings and things are made.

Deborah gloried most in her sense of herself as motherly matter on Sunday mornings, when she enjoyed an extended levée with Orlando. She could only think of motherhood as a triumph when she lay back among her cushions and caressed the feathery back of his neck while his jaws were working on her still streaky breasts. The exquisite, literally succulent, intimacy she enjoyed with her own baby – a creature whose responses were insensitive to the bodily blemishes that inhibited other human physical contacts – gave Deborah a sympathetic understanding of those women with swollen legs and bursting clothes who crowded out the ante-natal clinics having one baby after another.

From such benign heights Deborah could not help remarking the more dutiful postures of new fathers, and the relative paucity of their immediate experience of parenthood had been much on her mind of late. A correspondence with Lincoln Baker, who ran a couvade therapy centre in California and who had been an acquaintance in those far-off days in Papua New Guinea, had led to his visit to Nativities and to the rugby-birth experiment Vivien had witnessed. This couvade scheme had now progressed from a twinkle in Deborah's long-lashed eyes to a folder full of draft bulletins and plans for a couvade weekend. She hoped to promote the project further through her meeting with Leonie Baxter, whose columns reached many angst-ridden fathers, potential clients.

Soon after Cora left the house on the Sunday when Deborah had arranged to see Leonie, Gordon arrived to take his mother to one of the Alcoholics Anonymous meetings that were a condition for her parole from an old folks' home. Deborah then expressed some milk and set all in readiness for Vivien, who was to mind Orlando for the rest of the morning.

Deborah would have had herself rolled up in a carpet and shipped to Rome if she thought she might get a hearing from Caesar by doing so. Because she hoped Leonie might act as an unwitting kiteflyer for the couvade, she had agreed to meet her at the Cloisters. As an exclusive women's health club this was not neutral territory for Deborah. She did care deeply about her inner and outer health, but there was no narcissistic dimension to her scruples and the Cloisters was full of mirrors.

This female equivalent of the businessman's golf club got its name from the medieval-style swimming pool around which its facilities were focused. The rest of the complex was more Orientalist in feel: high white ceilings and archways, mosaiced recesses in which were tucked jacuzzis, saunas and herbal baths, and a relaxation area where exotic birds squawked and shat among tropical plants. It was a women's quarter of a recuperative kind, but on the 'members and guests only' Sunday mornings, the odalisques were no one's chattels.

Deborah was not comfortable in the towel handed to her

as a sarong, which barely girthed a figure that might have made her a Stone Age sex symbol, and she found it hard to avoid the mirrors as she stepped gingerly towards the swimming pool. Although Deborah expected Leonie to be punctual because she was religiously thorough about her Sunday devotions, she soon realized that she would have trouble finding her because the place bristled with tall, tanned and thin blondes. Still, Deborah supposed, reasonably, that Leonie would not have the same difficulty in locating her, so she slapped happily into the pool like a walrus sinking into a zoo grotto. She was lying on her back, dispersing rose petals with her fingers, when the light of the toasted-sandwich-maker of a sunbed on a balcony overlooking the pool went out. A lithe body jumped up and leaned over the railing. It was Leonie. The sunbed goggles had left a slight red mark on her nose and even when standing her hip bones jutted out like rounded little spires.

'Hi,' she cooed into the pool, 'enjoying yourself?'

Deborah raised one arm in a 'this is the life' gesture and Leonie came down to the poolside. With less Archimedean impact than Deborah, she slipped into the water and did a methodical breaststroke up and down the pool's length before retreating to the steps again in order to pat her face.

Meanwhile Deborah had heaved herself on to a swing, the seat of which was just, but only just, wide enough for her. Before she could remind herself of her vow of self-restraint, she was quoting Martin Luther: 'Women ought to stay at home; the way they were created indicates this, for they have broad hips and a wide fundament to sit upon, keep house and bear and raise children.'

'Luther was a constipated git.' Leonie scornfully kicked a stray rose petal with her foot and shifted her own narrow fundament, and Deborah felt warned.

'I suppose Viv's told you what I'd like to do?'

'Yes. It sounds very interesting and I have been giving

34

our relationship some thought.'

'She's not happy is she?'

'No.' Deborah sighed and the swing creaked ominously out over the water. 'She's not happy. She's never been a very realistic person and she just won't compromise with life.'

'How so?'

'You will let me see what you write won't you?'

'Of course.' Leonie flicked her crinkle-cut curls impatiently. 'I'm hardly in a position to take notes here. You just talk and when I've done something you can both have a look at it.'

Deborah clambered off the swing and sat down beside Leonie. 'Well, what I've been thinking is that Vivien still thinks she's going to find permanent orgasm with Mr Right, and since I've had Orlando I've come to the conclusion that women were better off in many ways when a baby was almost inevitably the consequence of having sex.'

'With a man,' Leonie reminded her.

'Yes of course, with a man. When women got pregnant involuntarily they couldn't carry on living like they did when they were courting.'

Leonie looked interested but not convinced. 'So you think Viv would be happier in a state of controlled misery with a baby as compensation?'

'Oh that's putting it very baldly.' As Deborah tried to rephrase her statement two other women arrived at the poolside, and since they were discussing a painful divorce Leonie suggested a sauna. Clutching her tiny towel, Deborah followed her as she hopped goatishly up a winding staircase and down a corridor lined with Greek male nudes.

'Actually,' Deborah said as she settled down on the sauna shelf opposite Leonie, 'I think my baby had a big effect on Vivien. She experienced something like sibling rivalry when he was born because until then she got most of what I offered by way of motherly love. I've always felt that sort of responsibility for Vivien because I got so much more out of our Mum that she did. Mum died when she was going through the rebellious adolescent stage. . . .'

'Yes.' Leonie interrupted Deborah by seeming to agree with her, although Deborah could not tell how intently she'd been listening as she hacked at her thighs with a wooden cellulite-shifter. 'It's very exclusive this motherhood thing.'

'Well do you know,' there was a great squelching sound as Deborah sat up on her shelf, 'that's just the thought that's been going through my head lately, and that's why I'm thinking of setting up a workshop for fathers.'

'What was Gordon like about the baby and that?'

'Oh Gordon,' Deborah shifted her sweaty body again, 'he's irrelevant and irredeemable. But even if he's incapable of confronting his emotional problems, I think there are plenty of men who'd like to.'

'So you feel on your own then, although I suppose his house is useful.'

'Er, yes,' Deborah hesitated for a moment, 'and Vivien and myself are Orlando's only family really. That's one reason why I wish she was happier because she'd enjoy it more then. Actually, she's babysitting this morning, which she hasn't done before, so I'm curious to see how she's got on.'

'How do you manage normally?'

'I've got a nanny, a sweet little Irish girl called Cora. She's very shy and very gentle and Orlando adores her.'

'So you're able to get on with your work.'

'Yes, but not like I used to. I can't be on call in that way any more.' Deborah was about to explain more about her couvade idea when Leonie directed her attention to the rivulets of milk flowing from her sagging breasts.

'Goodness,' Deborah laughed, 'maybe I could sell it to someone for a bath!'

But Leonie didn't laugh back. In fact she looked horri-

36

fied and Deborah could not help thinking that Leonie was punishing her pencil-thighs for fear that Deborah's own shape might be contagious. 'I've actually lost weight since having a baby you know,' she said humbly. But now it was time for Leonie's 'rejuvenating seaweed envelopement' and so Deborah lumbered off on her own to snooze on a leather-covered sofa in the general relaxation area. When the rejuvenated Leonie rejoined her, she had little difficulty in persuading her to come back to Chapel Grove for a light lunch and a look at suitable old photographs of the Lieberman sisters as little girls.

Deborah tried not to appear distracted by the full baby bottle on the kitchen table and the note from Vivien saying she'd taken Orlando out for a walk. Instead, she answered the door to Lincoln Baker and expressed delight at the amazing coincidence that one of her 'dearest' old friends was present. She introduced him to Leonie with another little coincidence which, to be fair to her, had only just come into her head.

'Leo,' she said, 'meet Lincoln Baker. Now you already have something in common through your surnames – Baxter's just an old version of Baker isn't it?'

Leonie smiled coolly and turned to survey Deborah's couvade-master. He was excruciatingly thin and if men can be told by their shoes, the archaeological sandals he was wearing on a proto-Spring day in London did not recommend him: they looked as if they'd been ripped off an ancient sacrificial victim recently dredged from a Danish bog. Lincoln's raspy voice went well with a decidedly unpatriarchal wisp of a beard. He sat himself down at the table, helped himself to some coffee, and after wiping his wisp on the corner of Deborah's lace tablecloth, droned over at Leonie: 'As women in western societies recapture the mysteries of the birth process, a complementary experience for men also has to be re-created. . . .'

'I don't see why?' Leonie's annoyance at having allowed

herself to be hijacked for one of Deborah Lieberman's impromptu little seminars was now obvious. Also, she was disappointed by Vivien's absence.

'It's a complementary idea, not something assertive,' Deborah continued, 'I'm not interested in taking anything away from women. But I do think that if men are required to be more committed as fathers in a total sense, it's perhaps not enough for them to be around at the birth. We can't expect men to change if we're always one step ahead of them.'

'What kind of men show up for this couvade stuff then?'

'All kinds.' Deborah made a grand gesture with her hands and her coffee cup rattled. 'Through mythology, ritual, dance, discussion and psychodrama we're rediscovering the creative, caring potential of the masculine.'

Lincoln took courage again. 'Many of the men who come to couvade groups are suffering from anxieties due to their having only been biological fathers in their past. . . .'

'You mean they don't even know for sure that they are?'

'Sure. But they feel unrealized because of that possibility. They might have been semen donors, for example, and then find themselves involved with a woman expecting a baby they really want to father, but find it hard to go ahead without absolving their biological carelessness.'

'Biological carelessness!' Leonie snorted, 'isn't this guilt-tripping likely to backfire a bit?'

Deborah shook her head solemnly. 'Some men just want to, or need to, go through the whole meaning of father-hood with other men to come to terms with things.'

But Leonie just gave Lincoln an even fiercer look, saying, 'In the good old days a fuck was good enough for most men.' Undaunted, Deborah laughed and, stretching out an invisible arm to gag Lincoln, she took the reins into her own mighty hands.

'Lincoln's experiments interest me because of the surprising number of men on our books at Nativities as applicant birth-mates. It's never been possible to fit them all in. Last month, for example, I met a young man who offered to play his lute and do massage. He'd got his girlfriend pregnant when he was a teenager and the baby had been adopted. But he hadn't felt able to get on with any other emotional commitment since, and thought that being at a birth might help.'

'Poor bloke,' Leonie commented, rather nonchalantly. But then she whipped a notebook from her satchel and asked if she could meet the desolated young lute-player.

'Well that really wouldn't be fair at this stage, but when I've arranged something for our couvade group, you might like to pop along and see what they get up to.' Satisfied that Leonie had been hooked, Deborah then directed the conversation into a coincidence that both her guests did find interesting, the fact that Lincoln had worked in the Gambia for a year, very near the place where Leonie and Marlene had taken a winter holiday. So while Deborah fretted about Orlando's well-being in his aunt's custody, Leonie and Lincoln compared notes on the cooking of Gambian-style chicken.

CHAPTER FIVE

A form of social apartheid operated in nineteenth-century London as those who could afford it moved away from the smoggy inner city to new leafy suburbs such as Clapham and Holloway. But from the 1960s onwards something like the pre-Victorian picture re-formed as the better-off recolonized grand old houses that had seen generations of multi-occupancy, and began once again to live cheek-by-jowl with the lower orders. Such proximity was feasible in the days of relatively full employment and the Welfare State, when the like of Deborah Lieberman could be sure of not falling over cripples as she placed her empty milk bottles on the doorstep.

What now remained of the long street called Chapel Grove, which gave a small hinterland of council estates, derelict terraces and a seedy high street its name, was still prosperous enough. The segment of late Georgian houses that included Deborah's was well-groomed by owner-occupiers of her own optimistic generation. But just one hundred yards away from this part of Chapel Grove there was a sociological Equator, over which Cora Mangan walked when she visited her brother.

Quite suddenly, the burglar alarms and window boxes, the forsythia bushes and Japanese lampshades gave way to a meaner, noisier world of thick nylon curtains and lidless dustbins, of empty beer cans wedged into struggling privet hedges and lean, constantly defecating dogs. The newish Renaults and Volvos gave way to untaxed and extravagantly cosmeticized Datsuns, and uninoculated children squabbled in the streets over cheap sweets.

Right in the middle of this latterday rookery was the Crown, a gaunt dinosaur of a pub that had resisted many ill-conceived attempts to lighten its dusty décor, or turn it into a wine bar. The Crown functioned as Patrick Mangan's club. Here he could cash the occasional cheque and receive messages from job contacts, and here he generally took his Sunday lunch. He was sure of the best of what was going when the manager's wife, Theresa, was supervising the catering, and when his sister joined him this solicitude was also extended to her.

After lunch, it was Cora and Patrick's habit to take a walk, which was often punctuated by Patrick's raids on the skips they passed. Skips, Patrick said, were a means for the redistribution of wealth. Unknown to him, this theory had been intimately borne out in the case of the furbishment of his own home. The preparation of a nursery fit for Orlando Lieberman had entailed the jettisoning of a load of perfectly good shelving and an old sofa bed, which, draped with a Moroccan rug, was a focal point in Patrick's boudoir.

Sometimes Patrick had the use of a van on Sundays and when this was the case he and Cora would venture farther afield, to Finchley for a 'rake' of old pallets and, once, to Epping Forest. But on this Sunday Patrick had no such pastoral outing in mind for his sister. When Cora walked into the Crown he was sitting with another man in his usual dark corner pew. While she sat down on the stool opposite her brother, he stood up and introduced his companion as 'Enda'.

Enda himself rose at his introduction and very politely expressed his delight in meeting 'Pat's sister'. He had a big, ash-grey face, like that of a before-man in a health education pamphlet. If people really are what they eat, this Enda was the very incarnation of rashers and eggs washed down with strong sweet tea. His spongey nose formation,

41

which reminded the studious Cora of pumice, suggested that he also took regular doses of alcohol, and from his shirt, which was open virtually to his navel because of a lack of buttons, a furry mat of grey chest hair protruded.

'Now now,' he said with a benevolent rub of great red hands, 'what's it to be? What are ye having? Same for you Pat?'

Patrick nodded and handed over his glass, but Cora hesitated.

'A mineral?' suggested Enda, 'or some pineapple juice?'

'No,' she said, 'I'll have what Patrick's getting.'

Enda hoisted up his trousers and went over to the bar. While he was gone Patrick told Cora he was 'harmless'.

'Poor bugger's a good plasterer when he's on the wagon. The wife threw him out a while ago, but he's got daughters about your age.'

'Where does he live?'

'He's got a place on the Fernwood Estate, and he's useful to them sometimes, or has been.'

'Oh,' said Cora, guessing that her brother's last remark must mean that Enda was more amenable than he was to occasional requests for accommodation for 'couriers', 'special deliveries' and so on.

Enda returned with two pints of beer and proceeded to pour some milk from a carton on the table into his own glass. For his ulcer he explained to Cora. Then, impatiently and authoritatively, as though he were a magistrate facing an exceptionally heavy caseload, Patrick got down to business.

'Enda would like to hear how Willy's parcel got lost Cora, because he can pass the information on to the relevant people.'

Cora noted the emphatic singular of Patrick's 'parcel'. Obviously, he had no intention of offloading the gun.

'I thought it was a load of brown bread and white pudding,' she began, under Patrick's stern eyes, 'it was all done up in loads of brown paper and string, and I think I must have left it in the bar on the boat.'

Here Patrick intervened to say, with overdone jocularity, 'you know, every little Irish girl carries brown bread about her person.' He was about to continue with some speculation about the spermicidal properties of brown bread but restrained himself when he saw how anxious Cora was.

'You see, I was helping this woman, Betty was her name, who had two children with her, a little girl and a baby. The last time I remember having the parcel was when I was with her in the bar, it was the only place where we could find seats. She had to take the little girl to the toilet so I minded her bags, and the baby, who was asleep in a buggy. Then, when the gangplank went up, I helped her off the boat and on to the train, so I think I must have left it behind on the boat. . . . I might have left it under the buggy.'

Enda gravely sipped his milk and glanced over at Patrick, who repeated, 'She thought it was just a load of grub for me. She wasn't going to go back and search for it.'

Finally Enda spoke, slowly and deliberately.

'It's really the ould uncle who's the divil in this. He should have checked things before entrusting a young gerrl with this kind of responsibility.' At this he smiled at Cora and she felt enormous relief, although she could sense that Patrick was irritated by her.

'In fact,' she said directly to Enda, 'she even gave me her address, where she was heading for, her sister's house. She said I could stay there if I wanted because the sister was going to the Middle East for a year with her husband.'

Enda now looked very alert.

'Betty?' he said. 'Did you find out her second name?'

'No. But the parcel might have got mixed up with her stuff because I did put things under the buggy when the baby was getting off to sleep and I was wheeling him up and down.' Cora was triumphant. She had forgotten these details until now and after rooting in her bag she did eventually produce a crumpled, crumb-dusted piece of paper with an address in Welwyn Garden City.

'I don't need it,' she said earnestly, 'I just took it to make her feel better. She wanted to show she was grateful for my help.'

Enda took the piece of paper and placed it in the pocket of the tweed jacket folded beside him.

'Well,' Patrick stood up, 'you've heard it all from the horse's mouth now. We'll just have to hope that Riordan's nest-egg went to some other worthy cause.' (It was obvious now to Patrick that money was involved.)

'I'll drink to that,' Enda wheezed, draining his milk, 'and I'll saddle up and go now. Don't worry your little head,' he said to Cora as he slung his jacket over his shoulder, 'and I hope you get into the nursing soon.'

With Enda departed Patrick was free to fetch their lunches from Theresa. When they had finished eating Cora meekly followed him out of the pub.

'Do you think he really will get in touch with that Betty?' she asked, trotting along behind him like the Emperor Hirohito's wife.

'No,' said Patrick as he slowed down for her, 'but I think it gave your story credibility.'

Patrick found his sister a bit of an enigma in a negative sense of the word. Years of being a poor relation in a string of households where her status was ambiguous, years that served her well at Chapel Grove, had left her with a frustratingly unreadable outer coating. It was never clear how much she understood, although Patrick, like Deborah, was not one to let another's ignorance cramp his conversation. Moreover, Cora was a great listener, happy to decipher the monologues at her leisure and sometimes, like a swearing toddler, capable of flinging things back at her instructors just when they least wanted to hear them.

As Patrick and Cora promenaded down the derelict streets that led to his home he began one of his little lectures. The topic was a favourite one, the status of people called the lumpenproletariat. A purely polemical term, Patrick said it was, for people who weren't in steady jobs, who didn't vote, who weren't even registered as voters, and who found diverse ways of subsisting on the margins of respectable society. People like himself, Patrick reckoned, voluntary outlaws. To Cora's horror, for example, he had not visited a dentist for twelve years. But he was in no mood now to upset his sister's civil sensibilities and the grim humour of the lunch wore off as he enjoyed a speculation on the Irish abroad, a subject Enda had probably brought to his mind.

'You see Cora,' he said as he wiped with his sleeve the tile he had just fished from a skip, 'our people never go back on the land, even in America. We're happier in foreign cities. This is like the Wild West and we're its urban explorers.'

'You're a Davy Crockett,' Cora smiled at the memory of a furry hat made from the belt of one of their mother's coats.

'You could say so, you could,' he smiled back at her.

'But you really want to go back, don't you?'

'I don't know at all, but it's tempting sometimes. Think of the lovely grass I could grow.'

That made Cora think about the crop at the hippy house in Rathbwee, but she didn't mention this in case it would bring on his bad mood again by reminding him of Willy.

'Maybe,' Patrick mused, 'maybe I will go back some time, when I'm thirty-five and I've found the right wee woman.'

Cora did not press him on the latter requirement. Patrick was mysteriously busy where women were concerned, mysterious because he rarely entertained them in his own place. During Cora's first weeks with Patrick he had gone off regularly with a blonde hairdresser who wore red leather trousers. Then there had been the Shelley whose van it was they sometimes had the use of, who bought items such as the tile Patrick was currently nursing for her stall in Covent Garden. There was also a likely erotic dimension, however historic, to Theresa of the Crown's motherliness towards him, and then there were the various women encountered in the course of his work building cupboards and shelves for the owners of newly converted flats. This train of thought reminded Cora of Deborah's enquiry as to Patrick's availability for the construction of a window-seat at Chapel Grove. She decided to ask him about that some other time. For the moment she was glad that the parcel affair was over.

Patrick Mangan lived on the second floor of a terraced house in Rochdale Gardens. This crumbling street had been evacuated of its original tenants in anticipation of its demolition by the council and most of them now lived in the grim Fernwood housing estate behind Chapel Grove. But financial difficulties and a successful campaign against the projected new road on ecological grounds, in which Deborah Lieberman had been prominent, meant that Rochdale Gardens was still standing three years later. The stalemate at the council gave the Rochdale Gardens squatters a semi-official status and although Patrick had lived in several different houses in the street, he was of reasonably fixed abode. He had become an expert at moving his domestic backdrop from house to house, and happily collected his mail from several hallways.

Patrick's street reminded Cora of the tinker encampments she'd fearfully scurried by as a child. To enter Rochdale Gardens was to enter an invisible compound encircling an open-air museum dedicated to the preservation of every alternative culture of the previous two decades. Smoke from painted wood, broken-up bannisters and cupboard doors issued from several chimneys and this malodorous fuel was usually gathered from the unoccupied houses by the street's womenfolk. Womenfolk, that was the right word for these beshawled and ankletted creatures, who seemed to Cora to flaunt their very downtroddenness.

These scrawny women were a far cry from the sun-blessed does who had graced the hippy house in Rathbwee. The seedy representatives of the urban species, they stood with folded arms and stared sullenly while tatooed men in cracked leather jackets lay prostrate under cars that would live to fight another day.

Patrick was sentimental about his community, but Cora was glad that his household held itself aloof from the rest of the street. The ground floor of his current home was occupied by a Rastafarian couple, Makeda and Nimrod. Their presence in Rochdale Gardens was only an episode, they hoped and prayed, in a trek that would eventually take them to Africa. Makeda deferred pregnancy and saved as much as she could from what she earned as a nurse in a local hospital. Her spouse, who took his name from the Nimrod who was 'a mighty hunter before the Lord', was indeed a very big bloke and he survived through a combination of film-extraing and cannabis-dealing.

The smell of Makeda's Sunday baking hit Patrick and Cora as they neared this house. But Patrick pushed his front door open to encounter some resistance and brother and sister squeezed into the hallway to find themselves alongside Orlando's pram.

'Shsh, don't wake him.' Vivien stepped out from under the bead curtain leading to Makeda's kitchen. 'I just thought I'd take him out for some fresh air. This is a really nice place. I hope you don't mind me calling like this? The door was open.'

Cora didn't know what to say. She didn't know how Patrick would take this. He didn't like people, especially women, presuming to call on him without an invitation. It didn't fit in with his outlaw image. But Patrick immediately took the wind out of Cora's anxious sails.

'Well now,' he said, almost bowing at Vivien. 'I'm honoured, I really am. It's not often that I have an opportunity of extending my hospitality to a Jewish princess. Won't you join us for a cup of tea?'

Vivien giggled and without checking Orlando she followed Cora and Patrick up the bannister-less stairs that led to his floor of the house. When she thought she understood Patrick's strategy Cora smiled to herself, for he didn't lead them to his large bedroom where he kept an electric kettle and the accoutrements for the simple meals he took at home, but to a virtually disused kitchenette at the back of the topmost landing. This foul stray cat sanctuary, in which there was still a functioning cooker and sink, acted as a decoy kitchen. Botulinium and salmonella seeped from its damp, peeling walls and the wobbly formica-topped table was stuck together with ancient grease. Cora thought Vivien would run a mile.

But Vivien didn't. While Patrick went off for some tea things she sat herself down with a contented sigh and gazed amicably out of the cobwebby window at Nimrod's vegetable plot in the yard below.

'Actually,' she said as she accepted a chipped mug of tea, 'I came round to deliver this as well.' As well as what, Cora wondered while Vivien passed a large yellow envelope to Patrick. It contained an invitation to a private view of Oceanic art objects at the Smithfield Gallery of Ethnic Arts, and the RSVP was to Gordon Arkworth, who Patrick had never even met.

'Deborah's probably got yours, Cora,' said Vivien, but that wasn't why Cora was frowning at her. Since Patrick's response was not as predictable as she'd hoped, to judge from the way he was fussing about Vivien's tea, Cora moved to a position of personal resentment at the invasion of her privacy. Sunday was her only proper day off, away from Chapel Grove, Orlando, Deborah and the whole lot of them. When Vivien enquired about a lavatory, and Patrick had directed her, Cora said in a sulky voice.

'She could have given me that to give you.'

But Patrick refused to see her point. 'Don't you see? It's specially for me in my capacity as a connoisseur of fine art.'

'A connoisseur of something else more likely,' Cora

48

snorted, and then to her delight a distant wail signalled that Orlando was getting tired of the fresh air in Patrick's damp hall. But Patrick disappointed Cora by suggesting that she and Vivien go back together to Chapel Grove, a suggestion that amounted to a command since it was, after all, his place and he probably had a date fixed up for himself later.

Lincoln Baker had left by the time Orlando and his entourage got back, and Deborah and Leonie were sitting in the kitchen looking through an old photo album. Deborah glared at Vivien after she'd picked up her extremely wet son and had a feel of the pram's saturated mattress.

'Leo,' she said, ignoring the sister whose potential virtues she'd spent the previous half-hour enumerating, 'this is Cora. She helps me with Orlando.'

Cora said a polite hello, to which Leonie responded by looking her up and down and asking, 'You're from Ireland aren't you?'

'I am.'

'What part?'

Cora hesitated and glanced over at Deborah who was making a loud tut-tutting business of peeling a wet pair of rompers off Orlando. Recalling Deborah's sarcasm after her last evasion of this unwelcome question, she almost whispered, 'A small place called Rathbwee?'

'Really,' Leonie looked impressed, 'where that siege was?'

'Oh yeah,' Vivien exclaimed, and then Cora scurried out into the hall to hang up her jacket. While she hovered out there she heard Vivien brazenly seeking her alienated sister's attention. 'You must remember Debbo, after Frank's thing. That's the place where they caught that IRA bloke with the funny name, the one who was involved in dope-dealing. . . .'

But as Cora re-entered the room Deborah gladdened her

49

heart by ignoring Vivien, and Leonie, and holding Orlando up. She prized his jaws apart and very emphatically addressed Cora: 'Look, he's got a tooth!'

Cora pretended to examine this tooth with great interest. In fact she had become aware of it days earlier, as a small white penny still barely visible in its gummy slot, but had thought it politic to leave the discovery for Deborah.

'I noticed it this morning when you'd left and I was giving him his cereal. I heard this little tap against the spoon.'

Leonie began to jangle her car keys. She yawned as she said, 'He'll be able to bite you back soon Deborah, and then you'll start worrying if he's on heroin or something.' And with that reassuring comment she allowed Vivien to usher her out.

CHAPTER SIX

The house on Chapel Grove was a strictly hierarchical machine for living. At its top was a converted attic, which served as Gordon's storeroom and also contained the as yet uncollected effects of Deborah's last live-in lover (whose books still lined one of the walls in Cora's bedroom). This attic also contained the small studio flat used by guests with some claim on Deborah and Gordon's joint hospitality. Below this was Deborah's floor: her bedroom, her bathroom and the room she called her solar, where she received her yoga teacher, important clients and close friends. As she withdrew from round-the-clock involvement with Nativities, the solar also functioned as Deborah's study. In the absence of a male in her intimate life, apart from the guzzling Orlando, these two top floors of the house were given over to cerebral activities.

Organic functions had the full run of the house beneath Deborah's suite – the nursery floor and below that, the kitchen. The great kitchen was the real throbbing heart of the house, to Deborah Lieberman what the Hall of Mirrors is to the French nation, the setting for many of her greatest triumphs and her bitterest disappointments. There she had stapled together those first Nativities mail-order catalogues and learned of her mother's death, and though Orlando had been born in the great bed of Ware upstairs, his struggle to be let out of his mother's pelvic fortress began as she paced up and down its polished floor in the company of her chosen birth-mates.

A riotous id held sway in Gloria Arkworth's basement underworld. Through a small door at the top of the narrow, creaking stairway linking her flat with the kitchen floor, she had access to the house proper. But it was repeatedly made clear that unless specifically invited, or forced by emergencies such as a shortage of ice for her whisky, Gloria was expected to remain below her rickety stairs. In practice this meant that she poked her head up over the trench only when Deborah's car was not parked outside and then she took full advantage of her ambiguous status in the household. Gloria enjoyed entertaining door-to-door salesmen, political canvassers and dealers in religious messages, electricity meter-readers, central heating engineers and mail-order delivery men. Anyone with a penis was ushered in by Gloria and off down to her own little kitchen, there to be warmed by a cup of tea, or something stronger, and regaled with stories about her days as the wayward wife of a Surrey tea-dealer. Inevitably, Patrick Mangan soon met Gloria in this way. He was immediately pronounced a 'lovely boy' and then the old lady stopped ranting about Cora's 'men'.

Deborah told Cora never to leave Orlando alone with his appointed grandmother. 'We don't want him to turn out like her son, now do we,' she'd say to Cora's discomfort. Meanwhile the Gordon whose mysterious faults were ascribed to his mother's failures as such was more concerned about Gloria's shoplifting and her drinking. 'Keep an eye on Mama,' he'd say as he set off on yet another business jaunt, 'and let me know if she's been doing a lot of her shopping.' But there was no need to protect Orlando from Gloria because, as Cora soon discovered, the old lady was quite indifferent to him. In fact, Cora found Gloria's downright callous attitude towards babies reassuring. While she knelt in silent awe at Orlando's yellow-stuccoed bottom, Gloria would rattle by with her drinks tray and snort, 'Shit at one end, noise at the other, they're all the same.' This reaction contrasted refreshingly with De-

52

borah's, who would have turned night into day on Orlando's behalf and who had once asked Cora to grate his carrots more lovingly.

As the non-aggression pact facilitated by Patrick's visit to the basement speakeasy developed, Cora decided that Gloria's early *faux pas* may have been committed under Deborah's eagle eyes when the old lady had felt it incumbent upon herself to show some granny-like interest in Orlando. In any case, as Patrick pointed out, Deborah had never given Gloria much of a chance. Orlando did not even carry the patrilineal surname. It was obvious that Gloria got on Deborah's wick, not just on account of her irregular visitors, but also because she had outlived Deborah's own beloved mother despite a lifestyle that outraged every modern prescription for good health. Gloria was only driven to seek medical alibis when her thieving threatened to bring police attention and Deborah's fully focused wrath down upon her head.

For all her security risks, Cora often found Gloria helpful as a decipherer of miscellaneous duties arising from Deborah's business. One morning, for example, Cora answered the front door to a short, bespectacled black man. This was Leander, Gloria scampered up to explain, Leander the womb-knitter's son. He delivered the expandable, open-necked woollen frames that, stretched over balloons, were inflated and deflated as teaching aids in Nativities active birth classes. Had it not been for Gloria, who also knew where to find the cash to pay him, Cora would have told Leander that there were no rooms to let in the house and shut the door, with possibly dire consequences for the national supply of knitted wombs.

But one other woman firmly allied herself with Deborah's tirades against Gloria, and that was Jasmine Roberts, Chapel Grove's cleaning lady. Once a fortnight or so, she came on a mission extraordinary, the cleaning of Gloria's flat, for which she was paid the equivalent of danger money. Even by Patrick's account, this was a

53

regular Augean Stables of a place. Though exquisitely, if eccentrically, groomed and manicured, Gloria's other personal habits were Tudor. She was, in Jasmine's phrase, a 'piss-in-the-milk-bottle-slut'. The local pest control unit had been summoned several times to deal with the fleas infesting her sofa (where the neighbourhood's most unsightly cats found sanctuary), the mice droppings under her bed and the cockroaches in her kitchenette. Jasmine was also under orders to purge the basement of any whisky bottles in excess of a Gordon-ordained ration of one a week, and she never finished her cleaning without emerging with at least one extra bottle.

One Wednesday morning, as Jasmine was donning her cleaning armour, Gloria surfaced without having been bawled out by Deborah. She was wearing an unusually sensible coat and with a suspiciously cute look in her eyes she asked Deborah, who was working at home that morning, if she could take Orlando out for a little walk. Cora was embarrassed by this request but to her great surprise Deborah agreed to it. 'Just to the high street and back, though,' she heard her saying and then she asked Cora to get Orlando ready. When Gloria had departed Deborah gave Cora an extra twenty pounds and suggested that she treat herself to something. 'Buy yourself some shoes, or have your hair cut. I'll be here and she knows she'll have to come back with him soon with me waiting.'.

Cora did not like going to hairdressers but Deborah's generosity hinted at a physical need to do so – 'rats' tails' would have been her Aunty Eileen's comment. So Cora forced herself to call in on Topiary, the local salon where the stylist of whom Patrick had had carnal knowledge worked. But that Lisa was having a day off when Cora asked for her and so she had to make do with the attentions of a tonsured young man called 'Samson'.

It was all so predictable. Samson lifted up a limp strand of Cora's hair with pseudo-scientific care and said, as she

knew he would, 'where do you usually get your hair done?'
Cora muttered her response in shame. Wasn't it obvious
that she didn't 'usually' go anywhere? She felt she should
rise from her chair and cry out, 'Forgive me Father for I
have sinned,' throw herself at Samson's sneakered feet and
swear that never, never again would she neglect her hair or,
God forbid, have a go at it herself.

The austere minimalism of the Topiary salon, with its
white walls and chrome furniture, went with its confes-
sional ambience. Cora's small face was completely drained
of colour when she looked into the mirror proffered by
Samson. After a long pause he said grimly, 'I'll try to do
something. Anything would be an improvement really.'

'Yes,' she said, biting her lip. Thereupon she was
wheeled away to the shampooing sink by a young woman
whose fringe bushed out from a bronze skull-cap. Meanwhile Samson continued working on a more faithful
parishioner. This lady had confessed to not having had
anything done for 'ages', 'at least six weeks', and confided
that her last stylist had been competent enough, though
lacking in 'inspiration'.

'I know what you mean,' Samson muttered caressingly
into this lady's ear while Cora's scalp was being mangled
by his assistant. After the wash she was left at the sink, her
head drawn back in a towel, like Mary Queen of Scots
saying her last prayers. But at last Cora's penance was
deemed done and Samson wheeled her over to the big
mirror. Snip, snip went his sharp little scissors and a rain
of hairs began to fall, some working their way into Cora's
nostrils and others beneath her vest.

She stared into the mirror and concentrated. Make me
into someone else was her silent plea, someone more like
the stony-faced girls with geometric profiles and Nefertiti
necks who adorned the salon walls. It was not that Cora
Mangan wanted to stand out in a crowd. Rather, she
desperately wanted to stand in with some group. She was
tired of being invisible. No one except Steve, and it had

been he who had first invited Cora there, had noticed her hanging around Rathbwee's hippy house, listening to its denizens' stories about colourful local characters such as her own rascally uncle.

Apart from its dowdy châtelaine, one Sadie, the girls at the hippy house seemed to Cora to have descended from some other planet. They came down into the kitchen at midday to make themselves breakfast, scratching artfully dishevelled hair and sauntering around with their thighs, thighs that had been bronzed in some hotter European periphery, visible under big cotton nightshirts. How Cora had longed to join that blissful, youthful Utopia. By day the hippies went windsurfing and blackberrying, by night, after huge meals that made everyone fart, they lolled on cushions, smoking joints and watching slides.

But even in London, where she herself was a visitor from another planet, Cora was still invisible. Orlando's pram put her at another remove. She was never stopped in the high street by the seekers of signatures for radical petitions, or given concessionary tickets for new nightclubs. Londoners often smiled at her, especially when she was with Orlando, but the world still consisted of groups of people and Cora felt alone, on the outside. Most alarmingly, it seemed to her that the city's alienating vastness was demonstrated by the existence within it of clones of all the people she had ever known. So much for one of the proofs of God's existence, that he had created millions and millions of perfect individuals, when every day Cora saw versions of her Aunty Eileen.

Once, on Patrick's suggestion, for he was a great believer in the social benefits of political activities, Cora had set off wearing new parrot earrings for a demonstration against the dumping of nuclear waste. She'd come home despondent and bewildered, convinced that though Patrick himself had been among the crowd he had not responded to her signals, and that alongside the march, draped with photographic jewellery, she'd glimpsed the face of the watcher-man.

The slight smack of the wet hair being combed against her cheeks jolted Cora into re-confronting Samson in the mirror before her.

'Oh dear no,' he said, shocked when Cora gestured timidly at the snarling blonde on a nearby magazine cover, 'I'm afraid your hairline is too low. You need a more defined face for that look. I'll just try to neaten you up a little.'

Cora didn't think she had Masai cheekbones but somehow she had hoped to look a bit more interesting after this ordeal, even if it were only an accident. She sulked while the brutally realistic Samson finished her off. Now Patrick, he was different, very defined as Samson would have put it.

'All right?' he eventually declared, pulling off Cora's towel shroud and summoning his assistant with another mirror so that she could survey herself from the back.

'All right,' she said flatly. She stood by the salon's glass door while waiting for her change and then she saw Gloria across the street. She was skipping alongside Orlando's pram, which was being pushed by a very tall, stooping man.

'That's Greta,' Samson said when he saw where Cora's attention was focused.

'Greta?'

'We call her Greta. She's our Garbo, a real ticket. She comes here to get the senior citizens' discount, but she doesn't have her hair done like any other pensioner.'

'No way,' Samson's assistant sniggered, 'and she tips well too.' That was a hint to Cora, who was still fingering her change and who now reluctantly put it into the box beside the cash register.

'Her name's Gloria actually,' she said sniffily.

'Really!' Samson exclaimed as he held out her anorak.

'Yes,' said Cora, still keeping one eye on the pair as they walked out of sight, 'she's a ticket all right.'

Once outside Cora crossed over the street and hurried until she could see Gloria and her escort entering the area's

57

only small park. Orlando must have dropped off because when they stopped to sit on a bench she saw Gloria pulling his blankets up and adjusting the hood.

It was an ugly park at an ugly time of year. The pollarded tree behind which Cora hid had all the charm of a dog with a docked tail. Cora's newly exposed ears were cold and she felt conspicuous because of her loss of hair, but she remained rooted to her vigil because even from a distance she thought she recognized Gloria's playmate. Was it the watcher-man in the khaki jacket who'd been hanging around in the vicinity of Chapel Grove ever since the day Patrick had come about the Luger? Or was it another man who to Cora's watery eyes looked like him?

'Who was that you were talking to just now?' she asked, as casually as she could, when she'd caught up with Gloria, who had said goodbye to her companion in the park.

'A friend.' Gloria gave Cora an unusually hard look. 'Don't you start blabbing to Deborah about my friends. Fat cow doesn't know a decent man when she sees one.'

'She is married to your only son.' That was the only reproach Cora could think of as she helped Gloria to get the pram up the steps to the front door.

'That tight-arsed little twerp was just right for her,' Gloria snorted, and then Deborah was on the threshold before them.

'Very nice, very gamine. You'll have to get yourself a new outfit now.' Cora was pleased by Deborah's immediate response to Samson's labours. She was very kind to her even if Gloria had a rough time of it. Something of Cora's old phobia about Gloria returned after the scene in the park. The old lady's promiscuity was worrying. When she met Patrick at the Crown later that week, she mentioned the incident. But Patrick was impatient and in no mood to listen. 'That just proves he's nothing to do with you,' he said, 'the old dear's pretty dicey, with that shebeen of hers. You'd never know what she'd be up to on her own account.'

But Cora still looked glum.

'Cheer up, have another drink. It might be your new hairdo. This watcher fellah just fancies you, and the old dear's his go-between. I don't suppose anything like that has ever entered your demented little head.'

Nothing like that had, or would, enter Cora's shorn head. For although it was true that she was often insensitive to male interest, she was quite sure that Chapel Grove's sentinel was indifferent to her hairstyle.

CHAPTER SEVEN

The crisis of modern art, its alleged symbolic aridity, was good news for Gordon Arkworth because tribal art objects were selling like hot cakes. Recently, he was even finding a small but respectable British market for his imports, and his latest exhibition was aimed at these home customers. Smithfield was a convenient location for the City men invited to the preview because their homes already featured totem poles and sand paintings alongside the grandfather clocks and vintage maps. Among them, Vivien Lieberman, wearing a fake crocodile-skin jacket and with her abundant hair raked into a Medusa-like nest by all sorts of ethnic bits and bobs, stood out like a drake among ducks. Several men gave her searching looks and said that they were sure they had met her before. But that was only because Vivien in full sexual combat gear looked very familiar.

In revenge for Deborah's mothering of her own ex-lovers, Vivien had become quite pally with Gordon and she had insisted on having Cora's 'gorgeous brother' invited to the opening. She had made Patrick Mangan's attractions explicit, and Gordon had been fooled, to make her interest in him seem like a purely objective, even a dispassionate thing. But, as Deborah well knew, Vivien had flexed her muscles and decided to seduce him, though that was not the right verb for a woman who handled all of her social relations with the subtlety of a country and western singer. Vivien fancied an old-fashioned sexual encounter with Patrick,

much like the health food addict who occasionally suc-
cumbs to a fried egg on generously buttered crusty white
bread.

Himself conspicuous among the finance ducks by virtue
of a denim jacket, Patrick helped himself to champagne
and then sauntered away from the crowd to examine the
sand paintings.

Vivien soon sidled up alongside him. 'Do you like this
stuff?' she asked.

'Not sure, maybe it doesn't work in our climate.'

Vivien twiddled her hair and drained her glass, whose
shape, she had just been told by a blear-eyed computer
whizz kid, was reputedly inspired by the shape of an
eighteenth-century vamp's breasts.

'Well it sells,' she said.

'I'm sure it does.'

'It is funny though, how the old capitalist genes break
through.'

Patrick looked at her enquiringly.

'I mean the Arkworths were quite wealthy people in the
tea trade and when Debbo and Gordon first got married he
told everyone it was their duty to squander everything on
the Third World.'

'Art and tribes,' said Patrick, 'and witch doctors.'

'Oh my sister doesn't squander things.' Vivien was
defensive.

'I never meant to suggest that she did,' Patrick said very
politely, 'but you have to admit that even this natural
hocus-pocus is big business these days.'

'So you disapprove of Nativities then?'

'Now that's putting things a bit strongly. It just seems to
me that it's a shame when we've managed to get rid of a
whole load of religious hang-ups, that more of them get
invented.'

'But we need to fill the spaces left by religion, at least
Deborah's clients do. They don't go in for big weddings
and all that, so they like to spend on the birth. We do need

61

new rituals, new symbols.' Vivien gestured at the scowling vulva-face on the wall beside them.

Patrick rubbed his chin thoughtfully. 'Why does money have to be involved? Why do needs have to become commodities? I mean, it makes the old religious stuff seem relatively decent. You didn't have to pay to go to Confession.'

'You mean about analysts costing a lot?' Vivien was annoyed at herself for having involuntarily recalled a wheeze she'd once used to get money out of her stepfather. She'd told him she was having analysis in order to clear writer's block.

'Sure,' said Patrick, 'and it's a terrible thing that Freud just ended up creating a new mythology which costs even more money.'

'Don't you think? Don't you think you might be being a teeny-weeny bit harsh?' It had been a struggle but Vivien had finally managed to get her flirtatious voice back.

'Harsh?' Patrick laughed scornfully, 'that's pure class hatred that is.'

'Oh,' Vivien squealed with delight and wagged a little finger admonishingly at him. Then she asked if Cora were as critical as he was, wondering on Deborah's behalf if the nanny were an enemy within.

'Good God no,' Patrick drained his glass emphatically. 'She doesn't think that way, not as marinated as I am I'm glad to say.'

The intensity of this conversation had separated Vivien and Patrick off from the general crowd, and Vivien now felt able to put out a direct line.

'It's nice,' she said abruptly.

'What's nice?' he looked searchingly at her with a grin on his face, and took her empty glass.

'I mean that some kinds of tension are really enjoyable, that's all.' He said nothing more but Vivien was sure that he'd got her meaning, sure that he'd deliberately brushed her arm as he wandered off to reload their glasses. But now

62

there were a few more brightly coloured drakes among the City ducks, including Leonie Baxter's painter partner, Marlene. She could be seen angrily thumbing Gordon's catalogue and heard accusing him of being a party to the scandalous side-stepping of native artistic effort: 'We can't afford exhibition space like this.' Gordon was his pinkest but otherwise not too uncomfortable. For most of the ducks, Marlene's outrage was part of the show. They loved to hear artists being angry in public. But Leonie left Gordon and Marlene to their debate and wandered over to join Vivien.

'How's it going?' said Vivien, wishing Patrick would return with her drink, 'that article. We haven't seen anything yet.'

'Sorry, it's in cold storage at the moment. Other things have caught up with me. But I've just thought of something you and Deborah really have in common.'

'Oh yeah, what's that?'

'You both indulge in man-redeeming fantasies. Yes,' Leonie glanced over at Patrick, who had been commandeered by Gloria and was bending over her while still holding two glasses of champagne, 'yes indeed. You've got your rough diamonds and Debbo's got her couvade men.'

Vivien smiled but said nothing. She was now presented with a dilemma about whether she should go to the post-opening dinner party at a restaurant in the West End. Gordon had indicated that Patrick would be welcome, should she wish it. But Vivien did not want to subject her dialogue with Patrick to Leonie's scrutiny. Then Gloria provided Vivien with the perfect let-out. To Gordon's genuine alarm, she was enjoying herself too much to leave as early as she'd promised. When Vivien volunteered to take her home, Gordon's new tinted spectacles glinted with relief.

'Viv, you're an angel. Take my car,' They exchanged car keys and Vivien managed to hang on to Patrick by asking him to help her get Gloria into the car. This proved to be a very sensible suggestion because Mrs Arkworth was quite happy to be settled into the back seat beside her lovely boy. And before Patrick could protest, Vivien had slammed the door on the two of them.

Only Cora's bedroom light was on when Vivien drew up outside Chapel Grove. She sent Gloria down to her basement and went into the big kitchen to make her an unsolicited non-alcoholic bedtime drink. Meanwhile Patrick bounded upstairs to Cora. They met on the stairway.

'How was it?' said Cora sleepily. 'Deborah's gone to bed with Orlando and I was just going myself.'

'Fascinating.' Patrick gently steered her back to her bedroom. 'Give me your essay and I'll read it over the weekend.'

'Wait there!' Vivien ordered him while she went off with Gloria's hot milk. So, putting Cora's essay on marine erosion to one side, Patrick sat in the kitchen fertility seat and leafed through a Nativities catalogue featuring such devices as V-shaped pillows for recumbent breastfeeders, lambskin fleeces, herbal teething powders, whale song tapes, and scented nursery candles, all of which had been tested on Deborah's own dauphin.

Although Vivien was now faltering in her original seductive strategy because she'd made the mistake of getting to know Patrick, she persisted in offering him a lift home. Then, once they were in the car again, she suggested he have a drink at her place. To her surprise he accepted.

'Your own place I suppose?' he said, once over Vivien's threshold and settled on a sofa bed with a glass of malt whisky.

'Yep,' she said as she cleared herself a seat beside him, 'bought with money I was supposed to finish my PhD with.'

'More squandering?' Patrick said this with a conciliatorily sheepish smile.

'Hardly. It's tripled in value since I bought it, and I did

give some of the money to a good cause.' But Vivien did feel guilty about the size of her flat, which had been bought to fulfil the inordinate *lebensraum* requirements of an ex-lover. As if he read her defensive thoughts, Patrick glanced slowly around the living room, finally focusing on a fading political poster in solidarity with Zimbabwe's struggle for freedom.

'You still active then?'

'No.' Vivien sighed. 'It's not that I don't believe in revolutionary change any more. It's just that I've lost my faith in people. Maybe I'm too old. I mean, what can you do, when all they want to do is knit bootees for royal babies.'

Patrick grunted amicably and chinked his glass against hers. 'I've never had much of a stomach for real activism myself.'

Vivien sat up straight. 'But you and Cora come from that place where the IRA siege was last year? A friend of mine, who's a journalist, said it was classic republican territory.'

Patrick sipped his whisky and tapped the sofa bed so as to dislodge the cat.

'Look,' he said rather severely, 'all around where I live now there are people who survive in all sorts of dubious and highly illegal ways. Some of them are semi-criminalized by the way they have to live, but it's the only way this racist state allows them to. So I don't particularly like pimps or turning a blind eye to stolen cars, but I wouldn't make it my business to expose my neighbours to police attention.'

'Of course.' Vivien grabbed her cat and stroked him protectively.

'Well, there you are then. The bed for the night, the blind eye. It's the same sort of thing, but that's not quite the same as complete political solidarity.'

'Sure,' said Vivien. She retreated from this subject by asking Patrick more questions about his immediate past. While Gloria had been dozing on his shoulder he'd whispered to her about his time as a residential social worker. 'So how exactly do you survive these days?'

'I'm a Pat of many trades,' he waved an arm at a lonely niche in Vivien's big living room. 'I build cupboards and shelves, could do something for that corner of yours for example, and I deal in post-Vicky bits and pieces when I find them. And from time to time I get rid of scrap metal.'

'Very busy,' said Vivien. Then she watched him rolling a joint with enough intensity to be sure of a puff. But when she took it from him it made her cough.

'Sorry. Should have made it weaker for you.'

'No, no. It's okay really. It's just that I haven't had it for a while.'

Vivien hoped he hadn't noticed the *double entendre* but he seemed preoccupied. They were silent until he asked abruptly, 'Do you ever get asked for carpenters?'

'Carpenters?' Vivien's hand went out again for the joint.

'Carpenters for the births?'

'Oh,' she laughed, and coughed again. 'No. Not to my knowledge anyhow, though nothing would surprise me. Someone could ring up and ask for a St Joseph stand-in one of these days. Last week Deborah got a call from a woman who wanted the works set up for her expectant cat. Can you imagine? Debbo referred the call to one of her unemployed friends.' Vivien moved nearer Patrick. 'Well, apparently, it was all set up – incense, music, the works – and then all the birth team got so stoned that they never noticed when the cat pissed off and had her kittens on the sly in the kitchen.'

But Patrick didn't even smile. Still, the dope was relaxing and as she slid off the sofa and on to the floor beside him, Vivien became aware of the pleasurable pressure of her nipples against her knees. She offered him some more whisky and when he declined she drank more herself and left him to the exclusive enjoyment of the next joint. But then he stood up suddenly and, rolling his shirt up and down his surprisingly tanned chest, asked her if he could have a shower.

'Sure,' she said, waving in the direction of her bathroom. He had been in there for about twenty minutes when she opened the door and threw in a large towel. Back on the sofa, Vivien smiled to herself. She was now so aroused by Patrick's presence that she was almost afraid, when he re-emerged and sat, patting his face, beside her, that her swollen nipples would take off of their own accord and implant themselves on his chest like shuttlecocks in a hedge. When she sneezed he grinned knowingly at her.

'The association between the nasal function and sexual excitement is well known. Sneezing in this circumstance is probably a consequence of the congestion caused by the swelling of the nasal erectile tissue.'

'Thanks a lot,' said Vivien bitterly, betrayed by her nose if not by her nipples and without any reciprocal sign from him.

'And what do you propose to do about it?'

'Oh,' Patrick stretched himself out on the sofa, 'I'm a great believer in pleasure deferment myself.'

That was too much. It was clear that he did not intend to sing for his whisky and Vivien felt weary of the whole caper. It had all been too smart, too knowing, and there was no hope now of a spontaneous fuck. They couldn't recapture the self-conscious opportunism that might have led to something two hours earlier. Vivien looked dispiritedly across the room, catching the heavy-lidded eye of the woman in the gilded poster on the wall opposite. One of Gustav Klimt's worldly ladies, she would never have found herself in this undignified situation. Vivien raised her arms above her head and issued a very theatrical yawn.

'I don't suppose you've heard of the connection between yawning and boredom, but I'd like to go asleep now.'

'Fair enough.' He seemed quite happy to leave without any ceremony and when Vivien apologized about not giving him a lift he said something censorious about drinking and driving.

'See you around,' she said as she waved him a dismissive goodbye.

'Yeah,' Patrick grinned down at her, 'see you around.'

Of course she would see him around. He seemed to be little Cora's only acquaintance apart from her dreary classmates. But was there any point in taking a special interest in Patrick Mangan? To Vivien's disappointment he was a more complicated person than she'd first supposed and now she found herself considering that he might be gay or, worse, that he didn't find her desirable. She cuddled her cat-comforter and finished off the whisky.

CHAPTER EIGHT

Deborah Lieberman would never have got as far as she had without what is sometimes called the Teflon factor. In addition to this professionally thick, non-stick skin, she had an effectively offensive way of weathering onslaughts on her integrity, and the integrity of her crusades. When Nativities began, for example, she responded to critics of her concern with mysteries of which she herself had no direct experience by claiming for herself the same status as those midwives, healers and witches of old who were also persecuted on account of their being childless, old, single, or all three. Deborah said she thought it 'interesting' that the very people who attacked her vocation went unblinkingly by the sight of a celibate Pope pronouncing on the most intimate details of female reproductive strategies.

But on the day when Leonie Baxter's article about the 'New Domestic Slavery' appeared, Deborah was momentarily vulnerable. She had spent the evening before at a dinner party animated by the vexed question of responsible parenthood in the event of a nuclear catastrophe. She had sat holding Orlando, whose sleep had been unusually fractured of late, among fellow guests amiably divided in their considerations on the grim options available. One diner proposed to kill his daughters rather than allow them to survive in a post-holocaust society; another guest referred to the possibility of emigration to in-laws conveniently placed in New Zealand. Deborah had been left with feeble suggestions about cottages in Wales, or Ireland, where she and Orlando could live on baked beans and play Scrabble. It had been a depressing evening and now it was a depressing morning.

Deborah told herself that she should have known better than to hit Leonie with the couvade project. Leonie's own relations with men, apart from her partner's ex-husband, were generally free of tension and uncomplicated. With hindsight Deborah realized that her couvade men would seem unpalatably and self-indulgently anguished to Leonie, who, moreover, was fond of Gordon and as friendly to Deborah's last lover as she herself was to Vivien's old suitors.

So the hoped for soft-focus sisters article had never been written and the promised photographer had failed to appear in Leonie's wake. Instead, the interviews with Vivien and Deborah had surfaced in a much less benign form. Leonie's latest article was an attack on those mothers who submitted to Genesis-ordained labours only to dump their babies on the demoralized nannies she quoted at length. Although Deborah was not named as a perpetrator of this 'untalked-of surrogacy', there was no mistaking the reference to the 'leading home birth guru who relies on a docile colleen'. Nor was there any doubt that Leonie's guns were out to blast the couvade project, for she ended with a butt at efforts to involve men more closely with the newborn. This sort of thing was merely an economic strategy: 'Only when a man has been bored out of his wits by the demands of a barely animate new baby can he be persuaded to fork out for the miserable wages of the mother substitute.'

When the docile colleen came downstairs she knew something was up because Deborah was still in her dressing-gown. While Deborah was on the phone to Vivien she had a chance to read the offending article, which was spread out over the breakfast table. As she entered the kitchen, Deborah sighed her 'Lord they know not what they do' sigh.

'You didn't really talk to her did you Cora? I should have warned you. Leo's a genius at hearing what she wants to hear.'

'No. She didn't talk to me at all.' This was perfectly true but Cora felt guilty about the article anyhow because it reminded her of Patrick's disapproval of her job. But Deborah knew that Cora was no mole. Indeed several references in Leonie's article pointed to the loquacious Lincoln. His presence around Nativities had become more and more of a liability as he took his couvade group on embarrassing, unauthorized exercises. Only the previous week he had been observed in a city centre chemist shop, explaining the feminine hygiene section to them.

'Honestly,' Deborah handed Orlando over to Cora, 'I do wish she had named me. I'd feel more able to defend myself.' Then, as a sign that Cora was exonerated from any complicity, unwitting or otherwise, with Leonie's attack, Deborah warmed up for her battling, declamatory mode.

'Honestly,' she re-proclaimed, 'the women of the Mutu Highlands involve every able-bodied person in childcare. We must be the only society in history where mothers are expected to be the sole companions of small children.'

Cora didn't say that was not the point of the article or anything like that. She held Orlando up and, wearing a practised look of alert sympathy, did her best to represent a rapt crowd of 50,000. But she wasn't good enough. Deborah suddenly grabbed Orlando back and began to insert him into a bifurcated outer garment. This meant that Cora was expected to take him to the baby clinic. Deborah resented the local clinic as yet another of the state's tentacles interfering in the sacred bond between mother and baby, and she usually took him for his milestone check-ups herself. But on this portentous morning it was only a matter of having his current weight officially recorded, so Cora could take him along. As she wheeled Orlando forth in his new all-weather reversible stroller Lincoln Baker was being ushered up to the solar and

71

Vivien's little car was drawing up outside the house.

Most medieval conceptions took place in the merrie month of May or thereabouts, a time, historians suggest, when couples could copulate in the relatively congenial, and often more private open air. In the huge Fernwood housing estate behind Chapel Grove some similarly uniform seasonality of birth, focused on Christmas, seemed to operate, although, faced with the grimness of the landscape around Fernwood, future historians would be hard put for the key variables. At any rate, this meant that the clinic was full of what Deborah called 'acrylic dolls in gender pastels' when Cora arrived with Orlando. By virtue of his teeth, his real hair and the ability to sit up that had prompted the purchase of the new buggy, Orlando was a senior baby among all the tiny Waynes and Dianas sitting on their mothers' laps in the crowded waiting room. The last to arrive, Cora was destined for a long wait and an hour passed before she was finally alone on the bench. While Orlando's throne-buggy, a limousine among all the other clapped-out baby transporters, was alone in the yard outside the clinic, Cora sat and waited for his name to be called out. She was extracting him from his snowsuit in preparation for this summons when a man walked in and sat down beside them.

'Who does he look like?' he asked Cora as he peered at Orlando.

'Like his Mum a bit, I think.' Cora thereby made her own position clear. Such conversations usually stopped when people found out that she wasn't his mother. But this man, still scrutinizing Orlando, did not seem bothered.

'Hmmmm, I don't know about that.'

He produced a plastic spectacle case, which Orlando immediately seized and began to bash against the side of the waiting room bench. It was only when the man rose again to his full height in order to woo this spectacle case back by offering Orlando a deal on an empty cigarette packet that Cora realized who he was. Rather, she still didn't know who he was, and she didn't want to particularly, but she knew where she had seen him before and she thought she knew what he represented. His outline was so familiar to her. He had that clumsy, stooping way of walking and standing which is so often the mark of very tall men, and now she was looking directly into his face.

He was very good looking in an old-fashioned way. That is, he was probably a bit overweight by contemporary ideals and his hair, which was brown and grey, was not fashionably severe but quite long and styled. He looked like a cleaned-up hippy. His wide mouth was slightly moist and as she listened to him cajoling Orlando into parting with the spectacle case Cora was struck by how very English he sounded, too English. He had a Mrs Minniver, pre-war, newsreel voice. You would have expected him to speak of wirelesses and gramophones, to say 'jolly good' or 'old chap'. He spoke the way Cora had expected more English people to speak, and to her galloping mind that wasn't surprising.

Hadn't Patrick, in one of his lectures, talked of the area's value as sleeper territory and weren't sleepers supposed to be integrated? According to classic Maoist formulas the rebel was supposed to be as a fish among water with his own people, and so the sleeper had to do his best to be an unobtrusive fish on dry land. Who would suspect this almost colonial-looking man, with his impeccable vowels and his hesitant, gentlemanly manner, despite the khaki jacket that almost dared you to guess his business? Patrick, with his black hair and his wild eyes and shabby clothes, looked the part much more than Cora's current companion.

She sat on the bench, frozen with fear, until she heard the name Lieberman being called out. Then she snatched Orlando out of his goo-gooing admirer's orbit and carted him off to the weighing room, staying there as long as she decently could. But when she returned to put his snowsuit

73

back on again, the watcher-man was still there.

'Good morning,' he said jovially to the nurse, who had followed Cora into the waiting room and was now shutting up the clinic. 'We're having a bit of spring weather at last.'

'Oh yes, lovely isn't it? Much easier for the babies too.' At this the nurse smiled over at Cora, who kept her grim face concentrated on Orlando's bootees. But while the watcher-man carried on his goody-goody act by carrying the nurse's bag out to her car, Cora managed to scuttle off down the road.

Now she regretted the new buggy. Deborah had bought it after an exhaustive research effort in which it had come tops for its capacity, among other things, to be braked in a gale-force wind, but it was not the *machine de guerre* that the old pram would have been. Still, Cora knew the terrain well enough to move fast. She knew the dips and uppers of every pavement within a mile of the house on Chapel Grove and as she rattled along the street Orlando let out a suitably piercing cry. But it was to no avail. The watcher-man was not even breathless with the effort of catching up. With his long legs he may not have noticed Cora's breakneck speed.

'You've lost something,' he said as he came alongside them, and stooped again to hand over one of Orlando's mittens. The sheer investment of physical effort necessitated by his great height made this transaction appear all the more gallant. Cora snatched the mitten from him but did not stop to fasten it to Orlando's left paw, or thank him. And then he must have noticed her panic.

'My my,' he said, 'we are in a hurry.'

'He's hungry. I've got to get home quickly.'

Watcher-man had won. He had managed to slow Cora down and get her talking. Now he asked her what had brought her to England, thereby forcing her to acknowledge that he knew all there was to know about her. She muttered something about 'giving it a try' and said something more about wishing to join her brother.

'Ah,' he said ruminatively, 'I suppose that was the natural thing to do.'

Cora did not find the courage to say, 'Go away and leave me alone.' So the remorseless chat continued. He asked her about her duties at Chapel Grove, whether she enjoyed her work and whether 'the man of the house' was about much.

'Not much,' she said, and then she bit her tongue. She shouldn't tell him too much and he had already asked her more questions than Leonie Baxter. But he was silent anyhow as they neared the high street shops and when Cora announced her intention of calling in on Ahmed's, he said 'cheerio' and disappeared like Alice's rabbit. Cora was left to negotiate with Ahmed without any cash. Since Gloria's recent interest in video cassettes Cora needed rather more of that than usual. On this occasion Ahmed had to be content with an entry in the little notebook Gordon had provided as a register of his mother's accounts during his absence.

Orlando started to wail again as Cora pushed him homewards and she wanted to join in with him. Who could she confide in now? Patrick was away for the week and recently he'd pooh-poohed her anxieties about the watcher-man. He refused to challenge Enda again and insisted on jokey explanations based on Cora's sex appeal. And although Deborah's suspicions about Cora's complicity with Leonie Baxter's plea for oppressed nannies had been fleeting, she dared not confide this watcher-man problem to her. Deborah's liberal conscience might stretch to the harbouring of a woman with unsavoury connections and a dubious past, but she would take no chances when it came to Orlando's welfare, and the watcher-man seemed rather threateningly interested in him.

As she stood in the porch Cora realized that she'd forgotten her key but while waiting for the door to be opened she managed to snatch the cigarette packet still in Orlando's grasp. That caused him to yell again, so Deborah picked him up and started to prepare his food. Cora went immediately to the lavatory, hoping for a few minutes in which she could calm herself down. When she came into the kitchen Vivien was sitting there with a smug look on her face.

'Has Lincoln left his usual visiting card then?' she said, beckoning at Cora to sit at the table beside her. 'Our recently departed couvade therapist, who is at this very moment, we hope, packing his bags. He leaves unsinkable turds behind him wherever he goes.'

'Oh,' Cora blushed.

'Yes, I'm doing a social survey on it.' Vivien turned to face Deborah and Orlando, 'You know Debbo you should have trusted my instincts all along. That Lincoln leaves his shit behind him as a sort of threat. Some people just bolt out of the loo and hope no one saw them go in. Others carry on regardless, and the conscientious people like Cora here, they try to flush them away.'

'We are not amused,' said Deborah, 'and Cora is embarrassed.'

'How did your geomorphology essay go down?' Vivien was proud of herself for so obligingly changing the subject and spontaneously remembering something about Cora's other life. The little couvade crisis had failed to distract Vivien from an uncomfortable obsession with Patrick Mangan. She was even having erotic dreams in which his naked body was deployed and though these fantasies were a source of some satisfaction to her, showing that there were some men about capable of arousing her, she longed for more control over her desires. Taking Cora's interests as seriously as Patrick did was one way of affirming some real connection with him.

'Okay I think,' came Cora's response. She was pleased by Vivien's enquiry. 'But Mr Leddy hasn't given it back to me yet.'

'I think it's really amazing that you can get it together, but I can't imagine what's so interesting about that stuff.

It's so dry and lifeless.' This careless follow-up undermined the charity of Vivien's original enquiry. Somehow, even Cora felt that Vivien's gush barely coated a suggestion that she herself was boring because her subject was deemed to be so. But Deborah rode in to her defence.

'Oh it's certainly not lifeless,' she said, jabbing Orlando's spoon in Vivien's direction. 'Rocks stand for permanence and stability but actually they're transient links in a long chain of geological evolution. In fact. . . .'

'Shut up Deborah!' Vivien rose to fetch a bottle of wine and gestured at Cora to find the opener. 'Let's drink to the disgrace of Lincoln. Now what were we on about before we got on to the subject of excrement and rocks?'

'Men,' said Deborah, unbuttoning her tunic so that Orlando could have his dessert. 'You were talking about an alleged shortage of men and I was trying to tell you that this hasn't been a demographic problem since the Second World War, in Europe at least, because the traditionally unfavourable discrepancy between male and female infant mortality no longer applies.' For the bewildered-looking Cora's benefit, Deborah enlarged on this speech.

'More boys are born, Cora, about 1,050 males to every 1,000 females. But because male babies are not as strong as females they used to die in infancy more often, hence the premium put on marriage for women, etcetera.'

Cora nodded politely as she sipped her wine.

'Well, well, well,' exclaimed Vivien, who was now gouging crumbs out of the cracks on the wooden table, 'where are all these fucking men then? That's what I'd like to know. Why are so many of my mates weeping into their cappuccinos? They can't all be on oil rigs or in the army?'

Deborah sighed and transferred Orlando to her other breast. Cora busied herself by sawing off wedges of bread and putting some cheese on the table.

'There are lots of nice men about,' Deborah began in her ever-so-patient, steady voice. 'My couvade men for example.'

'Oh,' Vivien snorted and reached for the bottle. 'I'm not interested in your namby-pamby nappy-changing wimps. I'm sick of foreplay and the new man.'

'All I'm pointing out,' Deborah's voice rose, 'is that there is no longer a demographic problem for heterosexual women but that doesn't mean that there isn't a cultural problem. It's possible that the male counterparts of your generation have not yet caught up with the women's movement and are therefore unacceptable. . . .'

'But I feel like a fucking dinosaur,' Vivien shouted, thereby making it clear that she did not want a rational discussion of her predicament. Deborah sighed and frowned at the little heaps of debris now on the table as a result of Vivien's gouging operation. She had long since run out of useful things to say to her sister about the sexual market, which she herself had felt well out of ever since Orlando's arrival. In any case, she felt that Vivien's very success in attracting men was her own undoing. She tended to pick men who were vulnerable in some way so that when she'd restored their egos by bestowing her attentions on them, they rose from their beds and walked away cured. Vivien also suffered from the I-wouldn't-want-to-belong-to-a-club-that-would-have-me syndrome. It was only a matter of time before she began to feel insecure about having made the first move in her relationship, to regret not having been wooed.

But now Cora, emboldened by friendly eye contact with Deborah, made an unusually firm declaration. 'There are more men on the land because women have to get work in cities and towns.'

'That's quite right,' said Deborah, almost patting her on the head. But Vivien was not impressed.

'What you forget,' she said, casting Cora a mysteriously vindictive look, 'is that more and more of them aren't even interested in women. I mean to say, time was when you could fancy film stars without feeling a complete fool. It's so depressing. . . .'

'Maybe,' said Deborah solemnly, 'but more women are finding other women to love.'

Vivien groaned. 'Women just don't turn me on. I'm bored by my wonderful clitoris. I like pricks.'

If Deborah's face now had its most disapproving, tight-lipped aspect, Cora's was pale and shocked. At other times she could take a certain superior pleasure in Vivien's inflation of the petty miseries assailing her, the Vivien who swore that she'd gained a few pounds in weight and considered retiring to a famine relief camp to lose them. But in the aftermath of her encounter with the chillingly chivalrous watcher-man, she could not feel so sanguine about Vivien's lament. It was as though Vivien were seeking precisely the kind of drastic sexual experience that had sent Cora to an abortion clinic in Richmond. In the silence around the lunch table Cora drifted into morbid thoughts about her own situation, past and present. Some-how, she was always stuck in the middle, neither a mother nor a proper nanny, neither a girl nor a woman. To this she added Patrick's diagnosis of the emigrant as neither flesh nor fowl, never quite at home in the host country and forever contaminated by foreign influences when back in the old country. Thinking about Patrick's ideas stirred Cora and although every non-combative instinct in her slight body told her not to engage with Vivien, she could not resist saying, 'My brother, he does well with women.'

'Huh,' Vivien grunted, but then she asked where Patrick was.

'In Wales,' said Cora triumphantly. 'He's building a sauna in a hotel.'

'Wales,' Vivien moaned with onomatopoeic intensity, but then she checked herself. 'Wales must be full of interesting men.'

This made Deborah laugh. 'It must be good to have a brother,' she said to Cora, 'It must give you a useful neutral perspective on men.'

Cora smiled distantly but appreciatively at Deborah, for

79

this remark reminded her of a similar utterance from the woman called Betty who she'd taken up with on the boat to England. After an exhausting voyage and myriad petty disasters, that Betty had cuddled her infant son and said, 'Still, you can't hate the men when you've got a son.' Cora was about to tell Deborah this appealingly relevant story, hoping for further approval and also, perhaps, insurance against the watcher-man's doings, when Vivien struck up again. She had had more wine than the others and Patrick's inaccessibility added to her bitterness.

'The thing that really gets me is that clever men can be quite happy with stupid women, and older men with younger women, but it's rarely vice versa. Most women seem to need to feel inferior to be comfortable in a relationship.'

'Oh that's complete and utter rubbish Vivien,' Deborah was firm, 'and you can't go round dividing the world up into clever and stupid people like that.'

'Hypocrite! You're always dividing people up that way.'

Deborah responded by plugging what remained of the bottle of wine and saying piously, 'you've got to learn to celebrate the differences between people instead of grading them.'

'Don't give me all that liberal bullshit, love your neighbour and all that. It's human to be prejudiced. Just by deciding that you love one person specially you're automatically downgrading the others.'

'That's no excuse. Anyway, people can change.'

'Not that much. There'll always be jealousy.'

'You're not really like this in practice,' Deborah gave Cora an apologetic glance, as if Vivien was a stroppy child. But Vivien lay with her curly head slumped over her arms and mumbled spitefully, 'I just don't want to grow fat and amiable like you.'

Now Deborah had had enough. She stood up and announced that she was going to her clinic, and Cora took Orlando off upstairs for a nap. By the time she returned to

the kitchen Vivien had left, and there was a sinkful of
washing-up to be done.

CHAPTER NINE

From the hour, on the boat over, when she had decided for definite that she was going to terminate her pregnancy, Cora Mangan had begun to make her own history. Then she had resisted Patrick by taking the Orlando-minding job, although that decision had had much to do with the immediate power of Deborah's personality, and something else to do with the beguilements of a centrally heated home after the rigours of boiling up hot water and fiddling meters in the Rochdale Gardens outback.

But now a cloud in the shape of the watcher-man had settled on Cora's self-determining horizon. She began to wake up shivering, and regularly searched between her sheets for traces of the doll-like, silent baby she'd been delivered of in scary dreams. Patrick had wrapped the little corpse up in brown paper and cast it through the open window to be caught by the watcher-man and dumped with an audible thud into his skip.

By day, the news heard from a shop radio that a baby had been sent flying to its death after a car had mounted the pavement collided in Cora's agitated mind with the bombing of fifty people in Athens airport. Soon, even Gloria noticed that she was looking 'a bit peaky', darting into the big kitchen one morning with an evil-smelling tonic. Deborah, too, who had been made more sensitive to her nanny's welfare by Leonie Baxter, expressed concern about Cora's loss of weight. 'Eat up,' she ordered her, 'or people will think I don't feed you.' As for Patrick, Cora's dream midwife, he was still inclined to dismiss the watcher-man phobia and more concerned about his sister's absorption into a household where she had no long-term stake. He took comfort from her commitment to the geology class and stood over her when she filled in the form and paid the fee enabling her to go on a field trip to Wales.

'Certainly,' said Deborah, 'I can certainly spare you for a few days. I'd feel better if you had a little break at this stage.' So, armed with Vivien's old camera, Deborah's pink Wellington boots and Patrick's binoculars, Cora set off from the same train station she'd arrived at. The field trip party was not a very scintillating one, consisting as it did of Cora's tutor and his two teenage sons, a retired married couple and an unemployed married couple. Patrick's oft ex-pressed hopes for his sister's romantic development were unlikely to find fulfilment among Cora's classmates, but she did feel that she belonged among them as she had rarely belonged before. Pushing her depression aside, she set off with confidence on each cold, wet day to examine bits of Pembrokeshire that were matched, jigsaw-fashion, by contours on the eastern side of her native landmass.

Cora's dedication to matters geological could have been said to have joined the odes of Keats, the *Lieder* of Schubert and Eric Clapton's *Layla* as the redeeming achievement of a hopeless love experience. To be fair to these artists, however, it must be said that Cora's interest had been stimulated after she had suffered for the love of a blond American youth. It had been Steve of the slender, hairless limbs who had first led Cora to a new awareness of a beach she had known since childhood.

Every other morning for nearly six weeks they had walked there together to gather mother-of-pearl and curiously shaped stones, which would be fashioned into the jewellery that Steve made. When they had collected enough material to keep him busy for a few hours, they

83

would sit down on the pebbles and stare out to sea. While Steve sifted small stones through his fingers, Cora would admire his feet in the sandals that he had bought earlier in the year on some Greek island. She listened eagerly to his stories about all the places he had visited, rarely talking about herself because she felt that she had not lived long or excitingly enough to have anything of comparable interest to relate. Later, she was to wonder what he would find to tell other girls about her as he continued his travels.

Sometimes when they were resting among the cushions back at the hippy house, Steven would drape an arm around Cora's shoulders in what she found a pleasurably proprietorial way. She would lay her head against his shoulder as they listened to Bob Marley in the jasmine-scented gloom, and hope for another move. But it never came. Although Cora was almost sure that she aroused him from time to time, because he would break away from her just when she was comfortable, he never made the move she was longing for, and he refrained from alcohol or indeed any substance that might have eroded this disappointing self-control.

As that summer drew to its close, Cora became impatient. Steve was the least intimidating young man she had met with and she wanted to be initiated into the rites of sexual love before the usual rucksack diaspora took place in autumn. When the other inmates of the hippy house began to talk of wintering in the Mediterranean Cora panicked.

Cora's rudimentary sentimental education was derived mainly from the sexy bits in her uncle's racing thrillers, most of which suggested that it was up to the woman to give the bold signal that the man was just waiting for. (Had Cora known Vivien in that momentous summer she might have been reassured that the timidity of men was not due to her own shortcomings so much as a wholly erroneous mythology of man as first-mover.)

One afternoon, when Cora and Steve had come back

84

from the beach to find the hippy house empty on account of a windsurfing expedition, she stood up between the floor cushions and took off all her clothes. Steve must have watched her doing this, but he pretended not to notice. He kept his head down and continued to twist little pieces of silver wire. Only when Cora sat herself down beside him, like the wretched woman in *Le Déjeuner sur L'Herbe*, did he raise his head to ask quietly, 'Why did you do that?'

'Why not?' she said stubbornly.

Without looking her in the eye Steve picked up her clothes and then Cora found herself raising her arms with all the wooden cooperation of an alienated toddler while he pulled her T-shirt back over her head.

'What's wrong with me?' she pleaded. But he just said, 'There's no need to rush things,' and she didn't have the courage to disagree.

Cora never saw Steve again. For a week she did not go to the hippy house, to the beach or to the crossroads where he positioned his stall on fine afternoons. When her will gave out and she did finally call and ask for him, Sadie responded crossly. The only permanent occupant of the house, which she ran on behalf of a distant tax-dodging relative, Sadie had recently suffered the loss of one of the goats whose yoghurt was sold in Cora's uncle's bar. This financial crisis was not eased by the fact that Cora's beloved had moved on without contributing to the household's kidney bean fund.

Cora knew that Steve would not return. Every time Sadie's van rattled through Rathbwee she went numb and every time she confronted Steve clones in American situation comedies the tears came back. What was wrong with her? She spent hours standing on a chair before her uncle's bathroom mirror. She didn't think there was any other woman and had never yet met a man with any alternative sexual preferences. No one in the hippy household had laid a claim to him. It was a painful, destroying mystery.

Soon, however, there was the consolation of geology,

first by retracing the beachcombing walks armed with an *Observer Book of Shells*. From there Cora graduated to her uncle's *Encyclopaedia Britannica*, which though too old to accommodate plate tectonics, nevertheless extended her interest beyond its original littoral focus. The time-scales involved were happily boggling. Landscapes had been roughly formed long before the advent of empires and Christianity. Rocks were therefore free of original sin or, as Deborah would have put it, they were for the most part pre-patriarchal. Alone on her beach on overcast mornings, Cora would enjoy the vindictive fantasies of the spurned lover. How she would meet Steve again on some other shore, where she herself enjoyed the status of the exotic traveller, and nonchalantly dazzle him with her scientific knowledge.

Willy tried to put a stop to his niece's scholarly dreaming by finding her more and more work to do. His intentions were good. 'Why don't you earn yourself a bit of cash,' he'd say as he came in with yet another catering assignment, 'and then go up to Dublin for the crack.' One evening, while Cora was moping behind the bar making pyramids out of matchboxes, Willy summoned her round the back. He handed her a packet of sandwiches, a box of eggs, a pint of milk and a stack of newspapers, and asked her to deliver them to the farmhouse her father had been born in. This was now the holiday home of a Dublin family, who had not been in Rathbwee since June and for whom Willy acted as caretaker.

'And not a word to anyone mind,' Willy barked before rejoining a salesman offering him plastic Georgian-style pub furniture.

The dog followed Cora out on to the road and across the fields deserted by cattle as the darker nights set in. As she opened the gate of the small and now derelict garden leading to the house a voice called out, 'What's your business?'

Cora turned to face an athletic-looking man of about

Patrick's age with lank brown hair and a half-grown beard. His submachine gun was not aimed at her.

'I'm delivering some things from Willy Mangan.'

The cigarette hanging from the corner of his mouth vibrated as he almost smiled at her and gestured with the gun at the front door of the house, calling out to those within that 'Willy's stuff' had arrived.

Two other men were in the kitchen. A very young red-haired man was bending over an upturned bicycle while his companion, older, fatter and with a circlet of black wiry hair around his balding skull, was studying the ordnance survey map draped over the kitchen table. This one looked up and smiled at Cora. Then he invited her to sit down and ordered the red-haired boy-man to make some tea. Cora declined but sat there while they ate the sandwiches.

The kitchen was neat and even cosy, in contrast with the hippy house kitchen which, despite cork tiles and a split-level cooker, still looked squalid with spilled muesli and overturned cat dishes. The rose-patterned washable wallpaper put up by Willy before the house had been sold was still there, as was the old shaving mirror high up on the wall where treats for Cora had been kept when she was a little girl. The kitchen had the aura of a cleaned-up cabin in the American Wild West and the three men, for the sentry had joined them for his ration of sandwiches and tea, looked as though they might be posing for the sleeve of an outlaw blues album.

The bald man sniggered as he glanced over the front page of a popular English newspaper, which had probably been left in Willy's bar by a holidaymaker, and the red-haired one leaned over him to find out what had aroused his mirth.

'Raging Bull Riordan in Gadaffy's Terrorist Holiday Camp' was the headline for a small article suggesting that several 'fiendish IRA hitmen' were sunning themselves in Libya.

'Now there's an idea,' said the sentry-man, rubbing his hands and eyeing what remained of the sandwiches to see if he was entitled to another round. 'I wouldn't mind at all. D'you think the tickets might be stuck in the post?'

But then Willy's dog began to snuffle plaintively outside the door because it was dark outside. The bald man rose and said that he himself would take 'the girl' home. They walked back towards Rathbwee through the fields, the dog over-excitedly running away and then circling back around them as he smelt the tantalizing wildlife smells of the evening. Cora's escort began to whistle, stopping whenever they heard the sound of a car on the road, which ran parallel with the fields. When he put his arm around her waist Cora made no protest. But she patted her head anxiously as she heard the chink-chink sound of the bats overhead because she still believed that they longed to entangle themselves in some woman's hair, which would then have to be ignominiously shaved off.

He kept his grip on her waist. When he told her she was a 'nice little thing' she said nothing, and she allowed him to gently push her against a grass-upholstered wall and kiss her on the mouth. She felt a thoroughly objective satisfaction with herself when she became aware of his body stiffening with desire, and helped him to lay her anorak on the ground.

It was as if Steve had been a creature from the Sun God's golden realm and this short, hairy man had emerged from some steamy underworld. Cora decided, in the same way as the faltering slimmer goes for the most grotesque cream cake, that she would seal her emotional fall from grace by having, or being had, by the least desirable man she had met.

In the dark he never noticed that she bled, although he was gentle in his own way. 'Do you want to know how I got my name?' he whispered when they had resumed their journey, as though he were conscious of having nothing else to offer her as a keepsake.

Cora nodded in the gloom, and stuffed her knickers into her pocket.

'It's from an American film that was showing where I did my first bit of fund-raising. Do you know it?'

'No, I've never seen that film.'

He giggled again and put on a voice she thought might be a parody of the red-haired boy-man's. 'But since, of course, the intelligentsia are unreliable, doomed to the role of querulous lookers-on who vacillate between anarchism and national-liberalism, I was really being very correct when I lifted three hundred quid from the Leeson Street Screen.'

'What's your real name?' Cora asked. But he didn't say and she didn't really mind. The silence added to her satisfaction at having at last joined the conspiracy of lovers who secretly populated the landscape around her. He wanted to walk her right to Willy's door, but she insisted there was no need and left him at the part of the road where the trees above locked together to form a leafy umbrella. About a hundred yards away from Willy's bungalow the dog suddenly bounded forward and then she saw her uncle walking towards her. He held his bicycle lamp aloft and looked cross.

'There you are. I thought you'd take your bike. Didn't anyone escort you?'

She linked an arm with his and then, hoping that its smell would drown out anything Willy might recognize, she accepted a cigarette to keep the midges at bay. She stayed in bed late on the following morning, worrying about whether she should agree to deliver anything else to the farmhouse if she were asked. But by the time Cora rose Rathbwee was swarming with Gardai and, a few hours later, with the journalists who were pouring in as fast as their hired cars would take them.

When the farmhouse was stormed all the police found were a bicycle, a packet of firelighters, a carton of stale milk, and some king-sized cigarette papers. Then, about

89

a quarter of a mile away, in the corner of a derelict old house sometimes used as a byre for calves, they found the red-haired boy-man. He had been unable to keep up with his companions because of a bowel complaint – too many egg sandwiches – and was taken off into custody with one clenched fist raised in a defiant salute. A week later, in another county, the police caught up with Raging Bull Riordan himself. He was shot dead while crawling through the ferns at the side of a stream. As for the third man, the talk was that he had made it to America.

Every woman in Rathbwee in command of a kitchen did well out of the unexpected extension of the summer bed and breakfast business, and Cora's hands smelled perpetually of the butter she slapped on to the sandwiches sold in Willy's bar. Although many people believed that it had been Willy himself who had tipped the wanted men off as soon as the police had come close, he did better than anyone out of it. He worked furiously to keep the journalists using his bar as their headquarters well lubricated: 'Come on now girl, get a move on,' he said to Cora when she came into the bar every morning, 'this is not an apparition of the Blessed Virgin. It's a one-off thing and we won't see the like of this business again in a hurry.'

Despite the cigarette papers that led to stories about drug-crazed IRA orgies, the journalists were disappointed by the siege's immediate outcome. A corpse was never as good as a captive. Cora could have made herself extra money by telling them how her deflowerer had earned his nickname, and thus forestalled some of the more outrageously pugilistic baptisms he received in print. But something bordering on a principled distaste for them stopped her. Of course, she felt differently when her period didn't come and she was grateful for a lift to Dublin with one of the media stragglers.

Cora's schoolfriends had dispersed to homes all over the country and the ones whose parents wanted them to know French were abroad in useless places. Sadie of the hippy house was the only person with whom she could have discussed her predicament from all sides. But to stop Sadie from adding her pregnancy to the catalogue of that Steve's deficiencies Cora would have had to tell her the whole story. That would have been too much for Cora's vanity, for she could not admit to intimacy with a man whose most unedifying corpse had been splashed all over the newspapers. Finally, she decided that her city-slicker of a brother would help her without asking too many questions. Ever sensible, Cora thought it wise, in the long term, to share her misery with a man.

Uncle Willy was strangely sympathetic and agreeable to Cora's sudden decision to join Patrick in England instead of starting the secretarial course in Dublin. 'Of all my clatter of sisters-in-law,' he said, 'your Aunty Eileen is the worst baggage.' Besides, he would be blamed anyhow for whatever direction Cora went in.

Somewhere on the route between Rathbwee and Deborah Lieberman's house, Cora Mangan had hardened and stopped asking God to shift fate in her favour. She had always given Him a reasonable budget and schedule, but it had become obvious that He was just another one of them. Anyhow, how could a divine being, whose personality at least was of such a short duration, a mere fraction of geological time, have true Cosmic validity? Cora had passed through a Sorrowful Mystery and come out with harder plating. As she sat in a Welsh pub surrounded by her geological classmates and ate sandwiches much inferior to the ones she used to make, she wondered if sex wasn't something like the insipid beer she was drinking. Something you had to acquire a taste for before you were unhappy without it.

CHAPTER TEN

Eventually Cora got over her reluctance to tell Patrick about the window-seat commission and he showed up at Chapel Grove to find out more about the job from Deborah. Her fondness for Patrick was more comfortably academic than her sister's. He was also glad to discover that, unlike most of his customers, she had a realistic notion of what the work would cost her and a healthy respect for craftsmanship, insisting on the best wood, brass fittings and so on. Deborah and Patrick lost no time in spitting on it and they agreed that the job would best be done while Cora was away on her field trip. During this time Orlando was to spend the greater part of the day with his mother at Nativities. His removal from the scene of Patrick's labours was important because he was now capable of moving, through a combination of bottom-shuffling and rolling, roughly in the direction he was least encouraged to head for.

'Right,' said Deborah as soon as Patrick and his tools were settled in the kitchen, 'I'll leave you to it then. Mrs Arkworth doesn't usually stir until about midday. Anything you need by way of tea or coffee, or lunch, you know where to find it. My work number is on the noticeboard if you need me.'

'Right.' Patrick mimicked Deborah's efficiency. She liked to get things done quickly. The only thing that had bothered her about pregnancy had been its duration, and she had outwitted biology by producing a baby of full term weight after only eight months. Now she carted Orlando off out of the room with loud, vaguely threatening assurances that his toy-cupboard-cum-window-seat would be ready within two days or less.

Patrick reacted to that ultimatum by downing his tools and lighting himself a cigarette as soon as she and Orlando were gone. He was sitting on the floor reading the foreign section of Deborah's newspaper when he heard the hall door being opened again. He put out the cigarette and began to whistle busily. Until Vivien walked in he thought that Patrick might have returned, to fetch something she'd forgotten or, perhaps, to make a not-so-subtle check on his progress.

'Oh it's you,' said Vivien contemptuously.

' 'Fraid so,' said Patrick, noticing her suspiciously madeup eyes, 'there's no one else about, apart from the old dear downstairs.'

'Shit. I'm not hanging around if she's likely to surface.' Despite this declaration Vivien took up Deborah's newspaper, glancing over the front page before bursting into tears.

Patrick paused in his work again. 'Something wrong?'

'Something wrong?' she shrieked back at him. 'Some bastard's just made a sardine can out of the back of my fucking car that's all.'

'I'm sorry. Were you in it?'

'No I wasn't. What do you think? If I had been I wouldn't be sitting here.'

Patrick sighed and turned back to his drilling. But he had to stop when he heard her saying something else. She looked balefully over at him and repeated, 'as if you'd care anyhow.'

'Now that's a bit uncalled for.' Patrick put his drill down. 'Make yourself comfortable and I'll offer you the proverbial tea and sympathy.'

'No, no,' Vivien waltzed to the kettle with vindictive gaiety, 'I'll make it. Make tea not love, that's our motto isn't it?'

93

Vivien actually made coffee and then she grinned at Patrick as he shovelled copious quantities of the sugar Deborah bought from some poor post-colonial country into his mug. She made a half-hearted attempt to find out about his work and he responded by calmly pushing a tendril of her hair aside and kissing her on the cheek.

'There, does that make it better?'

But this conciliatory gesture had a violent effect, for almost immediately Vivien was snivelling again, and she turned her head round so that she was soon burrowing into his waist. Between stabs at his navel with her tongue she croaked, 'Why does everything go wrong in my life?'

Patrick shook his head but kept one hand on the crown of Vivien's head. He couldn't for the life of him think what was seriously wrong with Vivien Lieberman's lot, except for the car, which was hardly an existential matter. But a precise account of Vivien's woes was not forthcoming. Instead she darted up one of her elegant little hands and pulled his face down nearer her, so that he was almost bent double when she kissed him enthusiastically on his mouth. Patrick made no attempt to resist and, still plugged by Vivien's lips, he gestured at the chaise longue opposite the area he was working in. They sat down and between nuzzling one another's faces they carried on kissing. This was good, Vivien thought, not dry pecking or slobbery sponging, but real, old-fashioned kissing. Perhaps it was his artisanal sense of perfection, or maybe it had something to do with plenty of practice in a culture where coital contact was deferred by months of mouth courtship.

'Mmmm,' she said, 'you've got a lovely mouth.' She touched his slightly splayed lower lip with admiration. 'It's like the underside of a mushroom.'

'In texture or chemistry,' he enquired, when he got a chance, and when she said 'both' he felt a slight disappointment because her ready answer confirmed his suspicion that Vivien's lines were a bit rehearsed. Suddenly she broke away from him, took his hand and said, 'Let's fuck.'

94

'What?'

'Not here,' she said with an irritation that signified complete recovery from the state she'd arrived in, 'up-stairs.'

'What about Mrs Arkworth?' Patrick only felt able to raise attendant difficulties.

'Even if she does get up within the next hour, she won't notice anything.'

Patrick fingered his spirit level gravely and said, 'Okay, but there's a condition.'

'Name it.'

'If I don't get this cupboard of your sister's finished on time, you can tell her that your car suffered an injury and that as some redress against patriarchy you decided to assault the next man you met.'

'That's the spirit,' she said, pulling him behind her up the stairs and into Cora's room, where the double bed was described as 'my old one' as an excuse for what she proposed they do in it.

They sat at the edge of the bed and then Patrick stared at Vivien in amazement, for she had stripped down to a black lacy camisole and french knickers. 'Never,' he said, shaking his head, 'never in all my born days have I seen a woman actually wearing that sort of clobber. Did you think you might get run over on the way here?'

But the saucy Vivien was businesslike as she helped Patrick to take his clothes off. Then they rolled together under Cora's floral eiderdown until she was sitting astride him with one of her hands firmly clasped around his penis. 'Oh,' she said with an air of some disappointment, 'you've been circumcized.'

'In the 1950s it was considered more hygienic, with the hidden agenda that it allegedly inhibited wanking.'

'I was just hoping for something new. I've never done it with a man who wasn't.'

That had a temporarily detumescent effect on Patrick, which Vivien did her best to compensate for, and soon they were rolling about again, ending up in the middle of the bed. There was no sound until Vivien directed his attention to her attenuated orgasm, which span round and round like one of Orlando's tops until at last it blurred into something her face registered as bliss.

But Vivien's sexual appetite was shamelessly egotistical. She was bored if her partner carried on for too long after she'd had her own climax. What had been excitingly frantic became a matter of indifference, only relieved by her fondness for the man in question or the possibility of re-arousal. For Vivien, the mutualist sexual etiquette of the 1970s, which so often resulted in male anxiety and the dragging out, or petering out, of male satisfaction, was tedious. But Patrick Mangan appeared to have an un-bruised sexual ego and so Vivien fought her desire to sleep, saying with the satisfaction of an industrious stallion's keeper 'I knew you wouldn't be afraid to stick it in. You're a regular Heathcliff.'

'And you fancy yourself as Catherine the Great, Lady Chatterley or whoever?'

'Something like that,' she said, snuggling unrepentantly into what she considered his pleasantly smelly armpit. The result was that they were soon at it again, and then they both slept. It was not long, however, before Vivien was back on top of him, gazing into his face and declaring his resemblance to the Christ Pantocrator.

'I'm Patrick Joseph Mangan,' he muttered irritably, 'not some vaudeville act.'

'I know, I know. It's just that I like a man to be a vehicle for my fantasies.' Vivien twiddled her fringe and lit herself a cigarette. 'Nothing like a post-coital fag.'

Patrick grunted and lay back on Cora's sheet. When Vivien stubbed her cigarette out on one of Cora's prized shells he winced, and began to feel nervous about this abuse of his sister's unwitting hospitality. He was pleased when Vivien gave him a few minutes of reflective peace by volunteering to go down to the kitchen and fetch them something to drink. She returned with a large glass of orange juice, most of which she immediately gulped down, and informed him that Gloria was up and about.

'I told her you'd gone out for lunch and that I was having a little lie-down on account of my headache.' This did not seem to Patrick a very plausible explanation for Vivien's presence at Chapel Grove in Cora's dressing-gown. But he said nothing and sat up to drink what remained of the orange juice while she dressed.

'What's wrong with your life anyhow?'

'Oh I don't know,' she sighed, 'I just don't seem to be getting anywhere. I've got loads of ideas but they never seem to take off.'

'Ideas are cheap. What do you really want for yourself?'

'I don't know,' Vivien repeated even more despondently, 'that's just it. You have to know exactly what you want, to be completely single-minded, to get anywhere. I head in every direction at the same time, and get nowhere.'

Patrick scratched his head and began to pull his shirt on.

'Honestly,' she continued, 'I really hate myself sometimes. All my energy goes into getting hold of money so that I can finish my book or something. It's so degrading.'

'Ah, poor you. Doesn't your big sister pay you a decent wage for helping out with the family firm?'

'Debbo pays me virtually nothing you know, and the bits of teaching I get are even worse. There are still so many things that need doing in my flat, and I really think I'm entitled to a holiday some time.'

'Well ask her for more money then.'

'I can't. I don't want to get too dependent on her. That's always been the problem. Debbo wasn't pretty so Mum had to make her out to be the resourceful intellectual one, with me as the bubblehead. I always had plenty of boyfriends: Debbo had to marry the first one, and now I'm left with nothing and she's got it all worked out for herself. She even looks better now than she did when she was nineteen.'

Patrick looked very solemn. 'My advice to you is the same as I give myself. Low overheads, that's what you should aim for. Don't need too much and then you won't get tied up, and you've got the freedom to do what you really want. You exhaust yourself thinking up stunts for that sugar stepdaddy of yours. Why don't you get a lodger into your flat? There's loads of room and that would help you to get on with the book.'

But Patrick had gone too far and Vivien was now very annoyed. She didn't want concrete advice, and who was he to give it anyhow?

'Where's your life of low overheads getting you then? What do you have to orientate yourself so carefully in aid of?'

'I'm not sure,' Patrick said without a trace of defensiveness, 'but at least when I want to make a move I'll be able to do it.'

'But you're practically a vagrant Mr Mangan. Look at where you live. That's no advertisement in my opinion for the value of low overheads.' Confronted with his silence, Vivien tried to get things back to some more amicable level. 'But at least sex is free isn't it?'

'Is it?'

Vivien looked at him, wondering if he could be referring to some complex idea about sexual exploitation, but decided, hoped, that he was just being teasingly enigmatic. 'Well, you're a tonic anyhow,' she said. Then she hugged him and they concentrated on a last virtuoso kiss.

After she had scampered off down the stairs and out the front door, Patrick rose from the bed and stood at the window's edge, just as Cora did when she was spying on her watcher-man. In the street below he saw Vivien opening her car and as she drove off he smiled to himself because it was none the worse for the accident she had invented to bring herself to Chapel Grove at such an opportune time. Then he lay back on the bed and waited for the sound of Gloria Arkworth's door shutting before descending to recommence his work.

Later that afternoon Gloria reappeared and offered Patrick a drink. 'That'll do nicely,' he drawled as she gave him a large measure of whisky, which he slipped more ice into every time her back was turned. When she asked him if he was any good at plastering he shook his head, amused by the range of functions he was being asked to fulfil by the womenfolk of Chapel Grove. But then Patrick had a useful idea. He did in fact know just the person to plaster the ceiling of Gloria's kitchenette, a person whose presence might kill two birds with one stone. He would introduce Enda to Gloria's job. That might rid Cora of her anxiety about the watcher-man and at the same time provide Enda, who owed money left, right and centre, with much needed cash. All in all, Patrick was pleased with his first day's work.

When Cora came home the cupboard window-seat, though still bare, was complete. Patrick told her that Enda was coming to do some work for Gloria while she was lining up rock samples along the mantlepiece in her room. Then he watched with some embarrassment as she turned to straighten up her bed. She lifted her eiderdown up in order to pull a mysteriously rumpled sheet and a small glittering object fell to the floor. Patrick nearly groaned.

'Look what I've found in my bed,' Cora said, knowing well whose diamond earring it was she was holding and now the reason why Patrick had shot up the stairs and into her bedroom ahead of her when she'd first got home.

'I went on a field trip and brought back some interesting samples, but I didn't expect to find any in my own bed.'

Patrick looked sheepish.

'For the love of God,' Cora continued on a high horse that was a joy to ride, 'can't you ever leave the women alone?'

There was no point in defending himself. 'You know,' he said with his most ingratiatingly brattish smile, 'I'm just like a lamb to the slaughter.'

CHAPTER ELEVEN

'Have you got an up-to-date passport Cora?' Deborah could be heard making this enquiry from the telephone landing near her bedroom. Cora was sitting on the nursery floor, consoling an Orlando who had been prematurely awakened by the ringing telephone.

'Not here,' she yelled through the open door, 'but I could write and get it.' Cora's international experience amounted to the one trip she'd made in the company of her arthritic Aunty Bernie to Lourdes, but Deborah was not seriously contemplating its extension.

'Don't bother,' she sighed as she bent herself over Orlando, 'you probably don't have an American visa or anything.'

Cora confirmed this deficiency with a shake of her head. She never knew how she'd be disappointing them. Deborah and Vivien, they were always asking for loans of the most unlikely things – foot massage oil and, once, a squash racquet.

As the rudely awakened trio processed downstairs Deborah fought Orlando off the front of her dressing-gown. She plonked him straight into his high chair and said, 'We'd better just give him his cereal and a drink this morning. I'm cutting out the morning feed.'

'That's quite sudden.' Cora's comment was carefully neutral because she now knew her place so well. She was Robin to Deborah's Batman, Dr Watson to her Sherlock Holmes, a person whose statements were the sounding board against which the thought processes of the more masterful personality could bounce.

'Yes,' Deborah offered her, 'it is a bit sudden, but I have to wean him some time, and I've been summoned to my stepfather's wedding party in the States. Sidney wouldn't want Orlando there. A grandchild, even of the step variety, would cramp his style. Besides, Orlando wouldn't really enjoy Manhattan, I don't think.'

Cora said nothing for a few minutes. She was regretting her lack of a passport because it might have meant an exciting trip and she was surprised by Deborah's acceptance of this invitation, or ultimatum, because she had always professed to be more independent of their stepfather's whims than Vivien. But Cora did pluck up the courage to mention, ever so delicately, her imminent examinations.

'Oh don't worry about that. As soon as I'm back you can have all the time you need. You can count on that.' That was all right. Deborah was scrupulously fair, even to inanimate objects. She used a different mug for her coffee each morning, 'to give them all a chance' and never wore the same pair of earrings two days running on the same principle.

'Maybe Patrick can come and stay with us?' Cora felt able to venture. She was a little nervous at the prospect of a period alone with Orlando and Gloria's presence was too intermittent, too unpredictable, to be reassuring.

'Why yes of course.' Deborah was pleased there was some immediate concession she could offer and since she did not know that Patrick was an unlicensed driver she said they could have the use of her car. But as soon as Orlando had been filled with porridge and become less interested in his mother's abruptly withdrawn liquid charms, Deborah began to look as flustered as she had when she'd first walked into the nursery.

'Come upstairs with me Cora and help me figure out what I can wear. I'll have to get new shoes I suppose, but I can't imagine finding a decent dress in time.'

To her many acquaintances Deborah Lieberman appeared to be happily bulky. She took pride in the fact that although she was undeniably 'outsized', she was also very healthy and quite fit. Her bedroom and the solar were adorned with celebratory images of the big woman, replicas of prehistoric figurines and baroque images, and she made uncompromising use of flamboyant clothes in much the same way as city planners highlight stubborn eyesores with gaudy murals. But despite a constant rhetoric about the tyranny of slenderness, Deborah under stress was given to bouts of self-hatred. The fact that her first lover and husband was a small, skinny man may have contributed to this discreetly ongoing anxiety about her size, though she typically managed to disguise her continuing shame by telling people that in her early married life she'd often hoped that she'd roll over in bed one night and squash poor Gordon to death.

By baring her body to Cora, Deborah was therefore baring a tormented soul and Cora did not know what she was letting herself in for when she agreed to vet the proposed wedding outfit. She and Orlando sat on a velvet-upholstered chaise longue in Deborah's bedroom, like clients at an exclusive couturiers, while various ensembles were pulled from a vast wardrobe.

Most of the clothes thus evicted and cast over the bed were dismissed by Deborah herself as 'too hippy' for Sidney's wedding party, which was a shame because the epoch of swirly long skirts and drawstring T-shirts had been her sartorial heyday. But of all the items offered for her serious assessment, Cora was most categorically horrified by the first, a rather severe, knee-length navy dress with a little white collar, the sort of thing fat women used to be told to wear.

'No,' she said decisively as Deborah tried to pull this little prison wardress number over her head.

Deborah looked at Cora as though to congratulate her for getting the first riddle right. 'I bought that bloody thing for Mum's funeral,' she said as she kicked it into a corner, 'so I couldn't wear it anyhow because he might remember. I have to find a real party dress and I have to look good for Mum's sake. Taste was the only thing she cared about, it was her form of morality. Do you know? The only time I ever really upset her was when I arrived back from Papua in my Mutu gear. She wouldn't even speak to me.'

Cora concentrated on the job in hand, squinting carefully at each thing Deborah tried on, pronouncing this 'nice' and that as 'not really doing anything for you'. It was tiring but when Deborah finally pulled a mustard-coloured velvet dress out of the wardrobe and slipped it over her shoulders, Cora felt able to sit upright on the chaise longue and say with genuine enthusiasm, 'That's really good on you. Wear that!'

But Deborah flopped down on the bed and burst into tears. 'It's not,' she insisted, 'I look like a Samurai warhorse in this thing. I wore it to the last exhibition of Gordon's I went to, and everyone asked me if I was pregnant. Anyhow, it's much too heavy for New York.' She picked Orlando up and began to dab at her eyes with the rag Cora used for mopping up his dribbles. 'What am I going to do?'

As the half-clad and tearful Deborah lolled on the chaise longue, Orlando gazing up at her with a questioning look, she looked like one of the Rubenesque beauties on her bedroom walls. She was Hagar with Ishmael about to be banished to the desert, appealing to Cora as the authoritative angel. At a sneaky level Cora enjoyed this role. She felt very calm and controlled as she picked up discarded clothes and sorted them into a neatly folded pile.

'We'll give these to the next jumble sale at the Fernwood Community Centre. I think it's silly to keep things you don't like and never wear.' Deborah just sniffed as Cora re-opened the purged wardrobe and began to fumble about for herself. 'Is there anything you feel really good in?' Deborah pointed feebly at a back top shelf and got up from the chaise longue to join Cora's rummage, while Orlando rolled in a hay of scarves and accessories on the floor.

'There's this,' she said, shaking out a tiered, multicoloured silk dress, 'but I've worn it so often. I wore it to Sidney's last wedding party and even if he doesn't remember it would be embarrassing if they take photographs.'

'Try it on,' Cora ordered.

Deborah pulled this wrinkled dress over her curly head and then stood like a suspect in an identity parade for Cora's inspection. But it was impossible not to notice that by fitting on this particular dress Deborah had unlocked the mechanism that told her she looked fine. The change could not be quantified. It was the same Deborah who had hunched up in the Samurai hoarding who now stood erect in this flimsy dress. Her whole face had lightened and she looked dignified and stately, priestess-like. Something positive had happened to her in that dress.

'Right,' said a relieved Cora, 'you'll have to get some material and copy it.'

'That's impossible. There's so little time and I'm no good at sewing.' Still, Deborah's voice had lost that note of utter distress.

'Maybe I could do it,' said Cora, examining the seams.

'Oh that would be wonderful,' Deborah laughed and rolled back on to her bed with Orlando. 'That would really save my bacon.'

By mid-afternoon Deborah had bought her material and Cora had unpicked the old dress to make a paper pattern from it. Soon afterwards Deborah pinned a large Nativities badge to her chest and set off to join a rush-hour 'sit-in' on the Underground, which was part of a campaign in aid of greater public sensitivity to the needs of pregnant women. The coast was then clear for Cora to beckon Gloria up to the seamstress's headquarters in the solar.

Since her recent acquisition of a mini cassette player

with bright yellow headphones, Gloria had been looking even more exotic than usual. Deborah unkindly likened her to those nouveau riche tribespeople who skip technologies and combine their organic clothing with digital watches and designer sunglasses. But Enda, who had arrived to start the plastering, gave no sign of being startled by Gloria. He had even mustered a certain graciousness when first introduced to her, and then they had gone off to take lunch together at the Crown. But once Enda had got all of his ladders into Gloria's basement and erected his scaffolding, the dust became too much for her and so she was happy to find something legitimate to do in the main house.

Helping Cora with her daring task appealed to Gloria, who saw herself as Rumpelstiltskin coming to the rescue of the miller's daughter imprisoned in the High Tower by the greedy king in order to spin gold from old rope. Deborah and Gloria's already brittle relationship had become more strained of late. So far as Cora could tell, this deterioration had something to do with Deborah's recent insistence that the telephone answering machine be left on when she was out. Deborah was generally out of sorts these days, often flustered and given to sudden decisions, such as asking Cora to remove the books from her room and place them in a crate in the conservatory, and the rather drastic weaning of Orlando.

So, while Cora stacked and re-stacked reels of cotton to keep Orlando amused and ran up and down the stairs with cups of tea and glasses of whisky, Gloria refreshed the skills acquired in her brief career as a proficient Home Counties housewife.

Vivien had been disturbed by a telephone call from America just before Deborah. She washed her face with soap and water, something she always did when fast thinking was required, leaped into her car and sped round to Rochdale Gardens. She rapped angrily on the front door until she heard a movement inside, and a sleepy Patrick, clad in an old trenchcoat, stuck his head out. He took a good look at Vivien's car and said.

'You've had the damage seen to then?'

Vivien pushed him back inside and up the stairs to that horrible decoy kitchen. 'You've got to help me,' she said, putting the lime-encrusted kettle on, 'it won't cost you a penny and you might even enjoy it.'

Patrick yawned and pulled his trenchcoat more tightly around himself.

'Please don't say no,' she urged him, 'it's my stepfather Sidney, I've told you about him. He's getting married again and wants me and Debbo, plus my fiancé, to fly over to the States for the wedding party.'

'Your fiancé?' Patrick's voice was still sleep-hoarse.

Vivien hung her head. 'A daft piece of inspiration that came my way last time I felt skint. You could say you're a restorer of antique furniture or something. Sidney likes people who work with their hands.'

'Hold your horses now will you,' Patrick stirred his tea, 'If I get your meaning right, you want me to masquerade as the fiancé?'

'Yes,' said Vivien happily, 'only for a week.'

'Why do you keep getting into these messes?'

Vivien looked crestfallen. 'I wanted to get the roof seen to on my flat, and I did give half the money to Nicaragua. Please say yes, you'd be perfect. If you don't say much you could even pass as Jewish.'

Patrick carried on looking tantalizingly solemn. 'You know,' he said, 'my Rasta friends downstairs think they're the real Jews. They can't believe that all these well-off white folks could really be God's chosen oppressed people.'

'Oh don't torment me Patrick.' Vivien walked over to push her soap-tautened face into his chest. Then she drew back and began to poke playfully at the dangerously loose button holding his 'dressing-gown' in place. 'You've even been done.'

'Jesus Christ woman,' Patrick snatched his coat from her, 'he's hardly going to inspect my balls now is he?'

'You will come, won't you,' Vivien exclaimed triumphantly.

'Hang on a moment will you. I'm not even awake yet. Just tell me, as slowly and calmly as you can, about the logistics of this operation.'

'Well, I'm to phone Sidney back this evening to let him know what arrangements his secretary should make. We can go by Concorde if you like.'

Patrick appeared to ignore this last carrot and slowly responded, 'I'll be your gigolo for a week, hopefully less, on two conditions.'

Vivien looked anxious again.

'That apart from my status as your fiancé with wings I tell no other lies.'

Vivien nodded.

'And we get booked into the hotel I want.'

Vivien was perplexed but not put out by this second condition, and she meekly followed Patrick into his real living quarters, where he rummaged for the address of the hotel in question in an old wooden filing cabinet. 'This is really nice,' she said, trying not to sound too insultingly surprised by Patrick's bedroom, which illustrated the maxim: never judge a man by his kitchen. Not only was it scrupulously clean, but it was also sensationally furnished along low-tech principles. The bed upon which Vivien sat boasted exquisitely white sheets (courtesy of a nursing friend) and had been made from varnished old pallets. The beer-crate bookshelves were loaded with hardbacks about mighty Britain's decline and around the hearth, where real fires burned on cold evenings, there were two sugawn-style chairs, their seats made not from slatted straw rope but from woven, flattened bicycle tyres. Most arresting of the room's many curios, however, was the rusty gun mounted over the fireplace. Vivien was standing up to examine this more closely when Patrick finished his search.

107

'Does this work?' she turned to ask him with a look of mild alarm.

Patrick laughed and put a faded aerogramme to one side. He lifted the gun off its mounts and stood back to draw with its barrel an imaginary Z-figure at Vivien's body.

'Not at all, not this heap of rust anyway. It's a museum piece, one of the original Thompsons smuggled into Ireland during the Troubles. Al Capone used a Thompson and this rattlebox belonged to my grandfather.'

'It still looks quite dangerous to me.' Vivien scuttled out of Patrick's firing line. Patrick shook his head and replaced the gun over the mantlepiece. 'You used to see them all over Ireland, in pubs and that, along with the horse brasses and cartwheels. . . .'

'They're not used now then?'

'Well, I suppose you could, but it would have to be in much better nick than this and where would you get the ammunition? Even if you had a good one, the bullets wouldn't even get through a modern flak jacket.'

But Vivien's concentration, always more hovering than fixed, had shifted to the bookshelves. Feeling completely at ease now in Patrick's sanctum, she boldly plucked out a book of photographs of Ireland. 'I'd love to go there some time,' she said wistfully, 'it does sound so romantic and I know so little about it.'

Patrick just grunted. 'But we know everything about you. Nearly everything that's printed, even that book, comes from here, and you know fuck-all about us. That's why we have to keep harping on about our history.'

'I wish you wouldn't say "you" like that. My grandparents came from Latvia you know, and so you're probably more British than I am.'

Patrick moved away from her with an indignant air.

'It's true,' she cried out, 'you drink tea and form queues, just like the English, and just emphasize these petty differences as a form of narcissism.' Since Patrick looked

108

quite impressed by this Deborah-like speech, Vivien felt able to continue more conciliatorily. 'It's like families. To assert your individuality you have to play up differences, but you're more the same than you're different. I mean I'm like Deborah in lots of ways ... and she's like me sometimes. Don't you ever feel like that about Cora?'

'No. But that's probably because she's automatically different as a girl. She feels more like my kin in a wider sense, and we've never been close enough to compete.'

But now Patrick waved his aerogramme at her and so Vivien closed the photograph book and sat down beside him on the bed. She conscientiously wrote down the address Patrick read out from the top of his aerogramme and watched without comment as he put it in the fireplace and set a match to it. When she called the next morning Patrick was wide awake. He insisted that she share some breakfast with him before they set off for town together to obtain his visa and a new suit, and when they returned to Rochdale Gardens Vivien spent the rest of the afternoon in his pallet bed.

CHAPTER TWELVE

Cora was not pleased when she heard that her brother was going to New York with the Liebermans. She found out when she was having Sunday lunch with him in the Crown.

'Oh I see, it's like that is it? It's Deborah this and Vivien that. You were the one going on about me being degraded, a slave and all the rest, and now it's okay for you to be all palsy-walsy with the great oppressor.'

'Don't be pompous Cora, it doesn't suit you. I know you're feeling a bit let down because by rights you should have the free jaunt, but there's a good reason for me to be going.'

'Oh yes? So I'm supposed to bask in your reflected glory as Mr Super Stud for Deborah's randy little sister?'

'Shut up! Stop being hysterical!'

'I'm not hysterical, and that's a really sexist thing to say.'

'Oh now,' Patrick whined and stuck his arms out to mimic an ape, 'sexist is it? Well now I never heard the like. Who's been borrowing the boss's ideas along with her old clothes then?'

Cora looked away from him and began to push Theresa's experiment with roast beef and two veg around her plate. There was a strained silence until Patrick said in a kinder voice, 'I didn't mean that really. It looks very nice on you.'

Cora sniffed and immediately plonked the elbow of Deborah's old jumpsuit, which she had ruched in at her waist with a wide plastic belt, in a puddle of beer on the table.

'You're still bothered by this watcher fellah right?'

She sniffed again.

'Well I got Enda to take some of the worry off you, but since then I've been doing my own bit of research and, between ourselves, I don't think the bold Enda is very relevant.'

'How do you mean?' Alarm had crept into Cora's watering eyes.

'Oh Enda's all right, but he's not really connected with anything, or anyone, any more.'

But Cora refused to be impressed. 'So what's this got to do with your going to America with Deborah and Vivien?'

Patrick leaned low over the table so that his face almost touched Cora's and whispered, 'I know someone over there, someone who was involved with Riordan's little sect, which, as you may or may not know, was not exactly kosher with the powers that be.' Cora drew away from him. She was distressed because of her uncertainty about telling Patrick that she'd met Raging Bull Riordan, to say the least, and confused because she did not know exactly what he was talking about. He looked slowly around their vicinity to check there were no eavesdroppers and continued in a less whispery voice, 'Riordan's gang were what you might call petty-bourgeois deviants – free love and hash, that class of thing. Now my friend, who I'm going to see, helped with the distribution of a certain consignment of illegal substances, not the hard stuff you understand, and he'll know what the botheration is about the money that's gone missing. You see some people think that Riordan himself made too much of a personal profit. . . .'

'What friend? Who is he anyway?'

Patrick sighed wearily and produced from the breast pocket of his denim jacket a colour snapshot. At the very end of a row of grinning men in donkey jackets, including a bearded Patrick, Cora recognized the man who had been the sentry outside the hideout cottage in Rathbwee. Patrick jerked a finger at this figure's face, from the smiling mouth of which a cigarette dangled. 'That's him, Dec Lacy. I worked with him on the Heathrow tube extension, and he's in New York now.'

Cora wiped her eyes with a sleeve of her voluminous jumpsuit and anxiously peered again at the photograph. Then, as Theresa came to remove their lunch plates, she smiled brazenly at her brother and said, 'What more can I say?' She had just about regained her composure and was taking a sip from a hitherto ignored glass of Guinness when Vivien walked into the Crown. She glanced familiarly at all and sundry in the crowded bar, practically pointed at the spotty chin that was her badge of association with the stubbly-chinned Patrick Mangan, and flung a set of car keys down on the table in front of Cora.

'It's all yours,' she said, and then Patrick explained that he and Vivien had thought it a good idea to give Cora some driving practice that afternoon. That was a way, he hoped, of sugaring the pill of his departure.

Vivien drove them out of the inner city and when the trail of dreary suburban high streets had petered out she stopped the car so that Cora could take her place at its wheel. Patrick's presence in the back seat made Cora more nervous than usual, even though he did his best to put her at her ease by seeming not to notice the odd crunch of the gears and by chatting nonchalantly with Vivien. Soon Vivien's grip on her seatbelt had slackened and as a quiet smile spread over Cora's face both her passengers lit up cigarettes. Cora was enjoying a strangely malevolent sense of herself as the powerful, grown-up driver of two lovebird victims. But this elation only lasted until they turned into the car park at the foot of Box Hill, where Vivien slapped her on the back with a violent 'Well done!'

The car park was crowded but a hundred yards along a woodland path beyond it no one else could be seen or heard.

'Come on,' said Vivien, 'let's play Jack and Jill went up the hill.'

'There's no room in that game for me,' Cora mumbled. She was lagging behind Vivien and Patrick because her moccasin shoes, which had served her well for the driving, were less serviceable on the damp, peaty ground. (Vivien had stowed a pair of Wellington boots for herself in the car boot.)

'I'm sorry,' said Vivien, turning round to wait for her, 'I didn't think.'

'She knows bloody well you didn't mean anything.' Patrick looked at his sister with exasperation and that decided her. She hopped over to a large tree and sat on her hunkers against its trunk. Then she gazed up at Patrick like a recalcitrant spaniel and said that she didn't think she could walk any farther in her light shoes.

'Oh come on will you. It's not too bad. There's no harm in a bit of mud is there? I thought you'd be into this sort of thing, acres and acres of your calcareous woodlands.' Patrick was desperately trying to salvage the outing's significance as Cora's compensation for his trip to New York.

'No,' she insisted. 'I'll stay here and wait for you and Vivien to come back.' She pulled a highway code pamphlet out of her pocket and sat herself down properly. Then Vivien sat beside her. As she tugged at the ankle of one of her boots she said gaily, 'I know, we'll all take off our socks and shoes in solidarity with you.'

'Don't be so fucking stupid,' Patrick flicked his cigarette lighter shut and put out a hand to restore Vivien to her feet. 'This is not a group penance. Come on Cora, get off your arse and come up with us.'

But Cora wouldn't be budged now. 'No I won't,' she shouted, 'piss off, piss off the pair of you!'

'Suit yourself,' said Patrick, taking the wounded-looking Vivien's hand and turning his back on his sister.

Cora stared fixedly at the highway code pamphlet until they were both out of sight. What a waste of an afternoon! She and Patrick could have gone somewhere more local

113

and less wet on their own, or she could have gone back to Chapel Grove and studied calcareous woodlands in comfort. She dozed under her tree for a while and then she sang all the songs she could remember to herself. She was rehearsing something crushingly sarcastic to say to Patrick when he and Vivien returned. Vivien's white jacket was grassmarked and Patrick wore his sheepish, suspiciously pacified expression. Stretching out her arms, Vivien proposed that they all run down the path to the car park together. But Cora, who was none the less careful to smile at Vivien while ignoring her brother, refused.

'That's our Cora for you,' said Patrick, 'always afraid to let herself go. She used to get off her bike and walk down hills instead of chancing a freewheel.'

Vivien laughed and tore off, and Patrick stumbled down after her. Slowly, Cora picked her way down behind them. He was right, she supposed self-pityingly, about her fear of living dangerously. Cora knew herself to be nearly always afraid, afraid of giving trouble. She had the right change ready for bus drivers in case of causing inconvenience with a large denomination note and even when no one else was about she sat at the edge of park benches. But her sense of injury was deepened by the fact that Patrick had offered this casually humiliating piece of character assessment in front of Vivien. It seemed that open disloyalty towards his sister was a measure of the fearless, dazzlingly greedy Vivien's status. Truly, there was no reward on Earth for the meek.

Vivien, meanwhile, was thrilled by what was for her a deliciously rare opportunity of being the kind and reasonable mediator. Although Cora regretted having presented her with this role she could do nothing but humour it. As she neared the car park she saw Vivien and Patrick crouching behind a bush but she allowed herself to be ambushed by them, and gave Patrick a grudging but acceptable smile of reconciliation. She took some chocolate and said that she didn't feel able to drive back, and so chirpy Vivien took the wheel. While Patrick dozed in the back seat she gabbled to Cora about the 'miles and miles' they had walked.

Within an hour of the departure of Deborah, Vivien and an exceptionally clean-shaven Patrick for Heathrow, Enda could be heard banging about in Gloria's basement. The temporarily stateless Gloria ensconced herself in Deborah's kitchen but when lunchtime came she went off again with her workman. Gloria kept finding more and more jobs for Enda to do and Cora didn't think Gordon would mind eventually footing the bill because the old lady had been doing less of her 'shopping' lately.

Cora's first day alone with Orlando went well. She dressed him from head to toe in blue in order to relieve herself of tedious enquiries as to his sex and told anyone who asked that his name was Jim.

'Jim?' said the woman behind them in the greengrocer's queue, 'that's a nice name. Eh, Lucky Jim!' Cora smiled and Orlando Evelyn Lieberman beamed up at both his admirers in complete approval of this betrayal.

When the time came to 'put him down' Cora solemnly bore him off upstairs and he tumbled into his cot without even a ritual protest. But in this model behaviour a dilemma lurked. How, Cora prematurely wondered, was she to reassure Deborah that her son had been perfectly happy without her, without at the same time implying that his mother was redundant?

CHAPTER THIRTEEN

Vivien maintained a passable to-the-manner-born expression during the flight to New York, a demeanour motivated by embarrassment at her sister's uncool enthusiasm, because Deborah was acting like a pools winner. Her chubby fingers were curled tightly around the champagne glass that she offered regularly for refills and she kept grinning at the Princess Di clone of a stewardess patrolling their section of the unexpectedly cramped aircraft.

Deborah did not like flying and she could only cope with this supersonic journey by lapsing into the little girl who had loved riding the Dodgems on Hampstead Heath at Easter. She had left her baby behind, gone on a crash diet and painted her toenails, but for what? Unlike Vivien, Deborah did not have any financial interest in gratifying Sidney because she had always made it clear that she had no need of his handouts. In turn Sidney had never acknowledged Deborah's success and his age and his world made him immune to her status as a minor celebrity. Even in terms of honouring her mother's memory Deborah had to admit that the trip didn't make much sense, for by Mrs Lieberman's criteria she was a failure, a fat woman who had, shame of all shames, 'let herself go'.

So Deborah concentrated on letting herself go. She strained round in her seat to vet the fellow passengers she identified as being possibly famous, giggled as she surveyed her gourmet lunch and exclaimed as she fondled a real linen table napkin, 'Ooh, it's all so deliciously infantile.

We're like babies in the sky.' She said 'yes please' to every extra helping of food and her handbag bulged with items of Concorde paraphernalia, including Patrick's disposable face towel. Then she caused a commotion by swopping seats with him so that she could get a better view and she sniffed her scented hands with rapture after an expedition to the lavatory.

All the while Vivien glared down at her well-manicured nails and sought solidarity with Patrick by occasionally casting him glances of weary resignation. But despite the fiction that had put him aboard that jet, Patrick was insisting on being with the two of them. He was amused by the sisters' role reversal, something Vivien herself had recently alerted him to the possibility of, and Deborah was proving to be a surprisingly entertaining companion.

'Business or pleasure?' said the immigration official at JFK, who, disappointingly, was just as ungracious as any other immigration official and not a specially laid-on Concorde usher into the New World.

'Both,' said Deborah with an emphatic hiccup, and Vivien added more coolly, 'we're here to attend a family wedding.'

After giving Patrick a long hard look, and consulting a computer print-out on his bird table of a desk, the immigration man finally shut Patrick's green passport and wished them all a happy visit. Deborah quietened down as they settled into the limousine sent by Sidney to take them to their hotel and as they cruised along the highway and over the Triboro Bridge into Manhattan, Vivien clutched one of her fiancé's hands.

The Biltmore was an old-fashioned hotel with mahogany-lined lifts and immaculately uniformed staff. Patrick and Vivien's room, which had been booked by Sidney's secretary in the name of Manganovich, was on the eighth floor, Deborah's on the sixth, so they said goodbye in the lift. Vivien went to the bathroom while Patrick tipped the porter. When she emerged he was stretched out on one of the single beds, with his shoes off and his tie unknotted. For a few moments Vivien also lay down on her bed, but then she sat up and announced that she was going back down to the lobby for some cigarettes.

'I thought you were giving up,' said Patrick mildly.

'I am really, but I have to have them when Sidney's around because he disapproves so much.'

Patrick gave his 'suit yourself' shrug and closed his eyes, opening them again only when Vivien returned. 'I had to ask one of the porters where I could buy some cigarettes and he said he'd get some for me. I suppose I'll have to tip him when he comes.'

'I suppose you will. You can't be the sort of person who jets in by Concorde and stays at the Biltmore and not be able to tip some cigarette-gofer.'

'I suppose not.' Vivien decided to be mollified by the fact that Patrick was talking politely to her. Ten minutes later an Irish voice outside their door called out 'room service' and Vivien admitted a porter bearing a silver tray on which her cigarettes had been placed along with a clutch of Biltmore-inscribed match booklets. She took the cigarettes and after rooting in her handbag eventually produced a dollar, for which the porter thanked her with a smart click of his heels.

'Imagine,' she said when he'd left, 'a whole dollar just for that.'

'Imagine,' came Patrick's weary reply, 'what that could buy you in this place.' Then he watched her until, like him, she was stretched out on her bed and said, 'remember, you'll be on duty soon as the good stepdaughter, so get some sleep now and keep your powder dry.'

About two hours later they were awakened by a phone call from the lobby where, as arranged, Sidney and his new wife awaited them. They had been married a couple of weeks earlier and the wedding party planned for that evening was by way of a social ratification. This afternoon

118

tea was an opportunity for Deborah and Vivien to meet the new Mrs Weiss in a more intimate circumstance.

'Hi,' said a short, tanned and neatly got-up man of seventy, who would have looked like a well-preserved sixty-year-old in London, 'it's good to meet Vivien's young man. Please meet my wife Sophie.'

Patrick shook hands with Sidney and then with Sophie, whose wizened chic matched that of her husband. Indeed both the Weisses advertised the benefits of regularly changing partners, exuding as they did an air of unrushed enterprise with the delicate whiff of their his 'n' hers perfumes. Sophie removed her gilt sunglasses, which then hung from the neckline of a silk T-shirt, and enquired as to the younger couple's 'happy day'.

'Well,' Vivien replied, 'we're not exactly sure yet because we have to wait until Patrick's divorce comes through. You see, they separated several years ago, but his first wife has been ill lately and he doesn't want to disturb her until she's completely well again.'

Sidney nodded understandingly. This explanation, which Vivien had rehearsed, was calculated to go down well with a man who was all too aware of the vagaries of ex-wives, the last of whom was studying computer science in Miami at his expense.

Before tackling black tea and an array of specially ordered 'non-dairy' cream cakes, Sidney and Sophie ceremoniously unscrewed the caps of various bottles of vitamins. Deborah took a great interest in all of this and then produced a photograph of Orlando, perhaps because she was feeling a bit displaced by the fuss made over Vivien and her fiancé. Although Sidney stared straight ahead, Sophie admired Orlando and even retaliated with a picture of one of her own grandchildren. That cheered Deborah enormously because it showed that Sophie refused to collude with the forms of self-censorship her husband had successfully imposed on his previous partners. It was also cheering that Sophie was the first wife of Sidney's since

Mrs Lieberman who appeared to belong to the same generation.

'I just love this hotel,' Sophie declared, 'you know it was Princess Grace's favourite.'

'Is that a fact,' said Patrick, who, as he had promised, had said as little as was politely possible during the encounter. As if she were reminding him of his commitment to a 'strong, dark and silent' mode, Vivien sighed appreciatively and, seizing his hand, pressed it to herself. This gesture was duly noted by Sidney as a sign of irrepressible young love. Patrick was aware of Sidney's appraisal and a little guilty about the whole deception because the dapper little man did not, on first impression, live up to the image Vivien had presented of an overbearing, reactionary tyrant who had virtually killed her mother. The approval seemed to be mutual because as they were leaving Sidney whispered to Vivien that she had got herself 'a fine young man'.

'I don't know why I didn't think of it before,' she declared happily as they got back into the lift. Then Deborah raised her eyes to heaven as the signal that the sisters' usual roles had recommenced.

Later that afternoon Patrick left the Biltmore and walked purposefully across Fifth Avenue and into Central Park. After irritating a few passing joggers by stopping them to ask for directions, he soon found himself standing beneath the statue of Columbus. He lit one of the cigarettes he had confiscated from Vivien and within five minutes was joined by the blond porter from the Biltmore who had bought them.

'How's the form?' he grinned, accepting a cigarette from Patrick, which then dangled precariously from the side of his lower lip.

'Grand,' said Patrick, 'not bad at all, and yourself?'

'Can't complain,' said the other, and his cigarette jerked like a ladder being adjusted against a window as he beckoned Patrick to follow him down a path, 'but call me Dick mind, I'm Dick Walsh here.'

'Dick Walsh?' Patrick's brow wrinkled as he searched in his mind for pertinent memories.

'Dead. He's dead, but I got his passport.'

'When did you come over?'

'Christmas. 'Twas supposed to have been earlier but Riordan fucked up the getaway.'

'How so?'

'Most of the contingency money went to some chick he'd knocked up.'

'How'd he manage that?'

'God knows,' the reincarnated Dick shrugged, 'randy bastard.'

Patrick lit another cigarette. 'Any idea who the girl was?'

'Search me, some local chick, that's all I was told. She wasn't a relation of yours by any chance. . .? Riordan was a right bicycle. The wife was expecting too.'

Patrick said nothing.

'Anyhow, your old uncle was the go-between, and if it hadn't been for that I would have been in California by now instead of tugging me forelock here for Johnnie-come-latelys like yourself.'

Patrick smiled and picked up the Biltmore cap his companion had kicked along the path in front of them. 'What now?' he asked.

'They've found a woman for me somewhere in the Mid-West, so I'm to be married soon and then I can chuck this lot in. But what about yourself? I never expected to see you in the Big Apple with two women in tow. Are you in the film business or something?'

'Ah no,' said Patrick, recalling how Dick's one-time accomplice had got his nickname, 'I'm doing what you could call a bit of charity work.'

Dick gave an appreciative sigh. 'I sometimes get to do that kind of work myself. There's a great calling for it from the women in these parts.' He then produced a couple of

121

cans of beer from his pocket and, as a sign of his integration, apologized for their temperature before offering Patrick one. They sat together on the grass until Dick redonned his cap and decided to go back on duty.

Patrick spent another half hour chain-smoking and talking to himself in Central Park. It now seemed possible that what Cora had mislaid on the boat was some compensation for her violation, which her uncle had secured for her. She must have unwittingly disposed of her own bride-price, a misfortune she could only be pitied for rather than blamed because she had surely underestimated her uncle's watchfulness and he had not thought to tell her of his delicate negotiations on her behalf. Images of brown bread and white pudding, and of smooth-talking American hippies, were now cleared from the deck of Patrick's mind. But one puzzling, and still worrying question remained. Who else had been hoping for a legacy from Raging Bull Riordan?

Near the Metropolitan Museum Patrick was jolted back into his immediate responsibilities by a loud hail from Vivien and Deborah. They were sitting on a bench eating ice-cream.

'Look!' Deborah cried triumphantly, 'look what I've bought Cora.' She unfurled a poster depicting a medieval St Peter perched on a rock. 'Upon this rock I will build my church. Don't you think that's just Cora?'

'That's great, really great,' said Patrick, sincerely delighted by Deborah's thoughtfulness, which was a comforting reminder of Cora's recovery from the mess she'd got herself into at Rathbwee. But Vivien licked her icecream sulkily. She had hoped that Deborah would suggest the poster purchase had been a joint effort. Now she goaded Patrick by asking, 'Why don't you nip over there and chisel off a bit of Central Park granite for her rock collection?' Patrick ignored this and sat himself down between the sisters.

'I'd love to live here, wouldn't you?' said Deborah cosily.

'I'm not sure.' Patrick didn't want to bring Deborah down by mentioning the busking flautist he'd recently passed, whose small child had held up a sign reading: MEMBER OF FAMILY IN HOSPITAL. 'It's okay if you're rich I suppose.'

'At the same time,' Deborah continued, 'one feels so grotesquely organic.'

'Oh, give over Debbo,' Vivien snatched Deborah's ice-cream, 'what are you on about now?'

Deborah looked only mildly aggrieved by the robbery. 'It's okay for you, you fit in. But I feel weird here with my leaky breasts and hairy legs, and everyone is so oppressively slim and fit. The young women look older because they've got so much make-up on, and such smart clothes, and the older women look younger. I'm just really glad now that I didn't give into the temptation to bring Orlando with me. Can you imagine changing his nappies at the Biltmore with all those beige carpets?'

Vivien groaned and Patrick squinted into the sun before suggesting that they return to the Biltmore for some iced coffee. 'And then I think we should all relax and attend to our ablutions for the do tonight.'

'Oh I do love it when you're authoritarian Patrick.' Vivien jumped up and linked her arm with his, and he muttered something about not wanting that kind of responsibility while, bringing up their rear, Deborah proclaimed, 'Every woman adores a fascist.'

Every other Monday evening Karen and David Zucker hosted a seminar in their Upper East Side apartment. Specialists on the digestive tract by day, they wished to talk culture and politics in the evenings. So they took out subscriptions to a hundred magazines and journals, and placed a want-ad in the *New York Review of Books* for partners in a regular discussion group. Sophie, who had once been married to a Bulgarian dissident-in-exile, was a regular at these evenings and at a meeting devoted to the state of US-USSR relations she had met Sidney, there on the slender basis that he had once been on a British trade mission to Russia. Over decaffeinated coffee Sophie and Sidney had discovered their mutual commitment to vitamins, and it just went on from there.

Appropriately, the wedding party was being hosted by the Zuckers and unlike several of Sidney's previous weddings the business associates usually drafted in from the highways and byways were outnumbered by Sophie's discussion group friends. It was a large party and the venue was the pier-level deck of a cruising ship moored at Battery Park. Although Vivien and Patrick had been nervous at the prospect of conspicuous status as representatives of Sidney's 'family', there was room for them to mingle fairly anonymously after the first ritual toasts. They squirmed only a little when Sidney bestowed a wedding blessing on them and, after being introduced to several of Sophie's relatives, they dived into the crowd.

The first person Deborah recognized, a burly real-estate man from New Jersey, nearly threatened her confidence in her new dress, her sense of finally having reclaimed her body from Orlando, by asking her when the baby was due. But when she looked startled, he easily persuaded her that he was just a little out of date with her affairs, had last heard news of her when she'd been pregnant with Orlando, and did not realize that the baby in question was already born and even weaned. Apart from this initial hiccup, she was destined to enjoy the wedding party, chiefly on account of Dr Karen Zucker's zeal for a subject that had always been hanging around in the back of Deborah's commodious mind.

'Deborah Lieberman,' the female Dr Zucker said as she advanced towards her like a prophet bowling out of the desert, 'am I glad to meet you. I just loved your piece on pre-Columbian obstetrics in *Witch*. Now what really interests me is the relationship between women and excrement.'

124

'I beg your pardon.' Deborah was not being unfriendly. It was just that she found it hard to believe her ears. Could it really be that this bona fide medic, hostess of her stepfather's wedding party, had read her article in an obscure publication and was now talking about what Deborah thought she was talking about?

'Shit.' Dr Zucker had read her thoughts. 'The last taboo. We can, and you do, say anything about sex and birth, but what about freedom for the bowels?'

'Women,' she continued as she drew Deborah away from a table groaning with vol-au-vents and plates of smoked meat, 'women have so much more trouble than men. There is the proximity of the anus with the vagina, and the menstrual cycle causes chaos. . . .'

'But surely,' Deborah looked wildly around to see if anyone was listening, 'surely it's all a matter of a healthy diet?'

'Oh no,' Karen Zucker shook her head solemnly, 'it's not. I'm surprised at you. Now what specially interests me is the incidence of what I call disorderly bowel syndrome among highly educated, professional women – liberated women. This has nothing whatsoever to do with diet, and I can prove it.'

'How very fascinating. But what has this got to do with my work?' Deborah's inhibitions wore off as she and Karen Zucker found a space of their own behind the staircase leading to the upper, uncovered deck.

'I can't tell you even half of it,' Karen Zucker's chiffon-sailed arms flapped upwards, 'firstly, having read your piece in *All-Women* about the dismay experienced by some women when they realize that bearing down is like having a bowel movement, and the connections you've made between constipation and difficult labours, I just knew I had to meet you. Sophie told me you'd be here for the party. . . .'

As Deborah warmed to her admirer, and the subject, the two women began to talk over one another in the excited way of old friends. Meanwhile Patrick was begin-ning to feel a bit spare, like a detective trying to hover unobtrusively about some vulnerable celebrity, namely Vivien. It was hard to be with her in any real sense. Far from restraining her, Patrick's presence gave Vivien the confidence to behave as she had never dared to before among Sidney's friends. Fortunately, Sidney himself appeared to have been well trapped by a nephew of Sophie's hoping for some venture capital out of the new connection, and so he did not observe his stepdaughter as she swiped glasses of Vermouth from the circulating trays, and ignored her minder's warnings about the disabling generosity of American measures. When Patrick finally washed his hands of her and drifted away, he first tried to join in with Deborah and Karen Zucker's conversation, only to be frightened off by its scatalogical nature. There was little he could contribute to considerations on the importance of human dung in medieval agriculture, the fondness of small children for their own faeces, folklore on the joys of farting and the deficiencies of western lavatory designs. So he moved on once again, enduring a painful conversation with a 'fellow' dealer in the antique furniture business before ending up back near Vivien.

Vivien's first chance to be unmistakably rude came in response to a harmless enquiry about what kind of shoes the Princess of Wales was wearing.

'I'm sure I wouldn't know. Suburban glamour doesn't interest me.'

She then deflected one of those compliment-fishing questions about whether she was enjoying New York with a lament about the absence of acceptable public transport. Ducking paeans to New York was harmless enough, but Vivien really took on the bad fairy's mantle when she decided to forget that, even in the relatively sophisticated company gathered by the Zuckers for the wedding party, a consensus of liberal values could not be assumed. Recalling a Zucker seminar on the subject, the husband of the woman interested in Princess Di's footwear ventured his opinion that a recent Anglo-American accord against terrorism was a good thing.

'Do you really?' said Vivien, arching her eyebrows and running her upper lip along the rim of her fourth glass of Vermouth, 'I actually think that terrorist is just a super-power word for people whose legitimate politics are denied legitimate expression.'

'Oh you do?'

'Yes I do. And, frankly, I think American political culture is a fucking disgrace, the most degraded ideology in existence. I mean to say, defining democratic freedom in terms of the right to carry guns, and squashing any country that tries to update the American dream with a bit of economic justice.'

Vivien's debating partner's wife was now clinging to him as if confronted by some ghastly spectre of international terror, and, as her tirade continued, Patrick became so agitated that he ripped a hole in the silk lining of his new jacket's pocket.

'What about the Soviets?' asked the real estate man who had stepped into the ring behind her, and she turned round to answer him. 'At least they generally pick the goodies to side with. Who can take Afghani freedom fighters serious-ly, for God's sake, people who stone adultresses to death?'

Patrick now resolved to do something. He thought about trying to faint, but that might be riskily dramatic, so instead he made another desperate bid to catch Deborah's eye. She responded by embracing Karen Zucker and bundling over to catch the tail end of Vivien's thoughts on Zionism.

'Darling Vivien, you can be so provocative. My sister's a dreadful tease you know.' Although the Russophobe looked less than convinced by Deborah's plea he did, perhaps, decide that Vivien was just a little eccentric and very foreign. 'You should come to one of our discussions,' he said sternly, as if one evening with the Zuckers would cure her. 'Oh if only we could,' Deborah said with dramatic yearning, 'they do sound so interesting.'

Then Patrick nipped in to snatch Vivien, leading her away and up on to the open deck. There he put an arm around her and forced her to take in great gulps of air. 'Don't undo all the good work,' he muttered into her ear with pseudo-loverly intensity, 'and lay off the booze.' Although Vivien flounced away from him and clattered back down the stairs to the main party deck, he saw her heading for the Ladies Room without waylaying any tray-bearing waiters. The trouble with Vivien, Patrick was thinking, as he stared out at the unreal lights of a papier-mâché Manhattan, was that she made up the rules as she went along without informing her team-mates. But Deborah was now working very hard. Patrick heard her telling someone that the Princess of Wales was now wearing stilettos and when the band finally struck up, she was to be seen doing a commendable polka to 'A Fine Romance' with Dr David Zucker.

At one o'clock in the morning, when their limousine had drawn up outside the Biltmore and Dick Walsh had opened its door, Vivien suggested that she and Patrick take a stroll. 'It might sober me up a bit,' she said and Patrick was inclined to agree. Deborah said she was going straight to bed because she felt 'a bit funny'. Vivien snuggled into Patrick's side as they ambled up Fifth Avenue.

'You were really super Patrick. You looked perfect and behaved impeccably. Sidney never liked Gordon because he's so cold and WASP, but you were just right. I began to think it might be fun to marry you after all.'

'Did you now. I'm really honoured, I really am.' Despite his sarcasm, Patrick refrained from any post-mortem on her performance, although the cardboard-box shrouded bodies he glimpsed in the exclusive shop doorways vindicated some of her outrageousness.

'Why,' he asked suddenly, 'why did your sister fall for someone like Gordon?'

'Oh I don't know.' Vivien detached herself from Patrick's side, a sign that this enquiry was an unwelcome intrusion into happier thoughts. 'She does have a masochistic streak in her, and Gordon was so unlike her. She used to write me miserable letters from Papua, telling me about various native drugs she was putting in his food to make him more randy and that.' Then she turned and took Patrick's arm again. 'Anyhow, Sidney said he'd buy us a house when we get married.'

'Now look,' Patrick turned round and steered them back towards the Biltmore, 'I've had my fill of this caper. I told you I'd only come here on condition this was the end of the lies. You should really think about getting completely away from the old geezer's power, especially now that he's got a new wife to distract him for a bit. Why can't you be more like Deborah?'

'But Deborah doesn't need Sidney like I do.'

But the party had convinced Patrick that Sidney needed the sisters as his quasi-daughters more than they needed him. 'We don't need him,' he said emphatically, and Vivien looked hard at him. Had he really said 'we'? She didn't notice Dick Walsh smirking as she and Patrick walked into the Biltmore lobby. Patrick took their bedroom key and pushed the door open with some solemnity. Then he gladdened Vivien's heart even more by turning off the main light and pushing the two single beds together. Vivien peeled her tights off and watched him fondly as he removed his linen suit and carefully hung it up in the wardrobe. They were enjoying what had become a ritual bout of steady kissing when the telephone rang.

'Fucking shit. Leave it alone. It's probably a wrong number.'

But Patrick insisted on answering and then he passed the phone to Vivien. A very miserable and deflated Deborah was on the line. 'I haven't had so much to drink since

129

before I was pregnant,' she moaned, although her problem was due not so much to a surfeit of alcohol as a lack of food, for she had had no opportunity of availing herself of the wedding feast. Her room was in a desperate state when Vivien reached it. All the belongings she had brought with her, including a small packet of disposable nappies, were strewn across the beige floor, and the shower tap was dripping noisily.

'You shouldn't have had so much to drink,' said Vivien as an unscathed pot to a black kettle, 'I'll see if I can get room service to bring you some coffee, shall I?'

'Rosie was right,' Deborah whispered, 'she said it was in my stars that something heavy would happen this weekend. That's partly why I agreed to go away.'

'That's absolute bullshit. You've said yourself that Rosie's predictions have been less and less reliable since she's had that computer Frank got her. You just need to drink lots before you crash out.' But a fresh glance at Deborah persuaded Vivien to be more compassionate. 'Honestly, Debbo, it's only a hangover. I get them all the time.'

'It's not a hangover, it's the curse. That's what's wrong with me. I shouldn't have dropped Orlando's last feed.'

This revelation startled Vivien. 'You should have told me first.'

'I didn't know when I rang you. I've only just found out that's why I've been feeling so peculiar. I thought it might be jet-lag or something, and I don't have anything with me. I'm using the nappies I packed by accident.'

Vivien burst out laughing, which forced Deborah to smile. She then dissuaded her from making an emotional phone call to Cora on the grounds that she'd be even more upset if she happened to ring when Orlando was crying, and got her to climb into her nappy-lined bed. Vivien had propped up the pillows around Deborah and tucked her in when another Biltmore porter arrived with a tray of coffee. As she left the room Deborah's recovery from the shocking

130

consequence of Orlando's weaning was marked by loud ruminations.

'Poor Vivien, poor us. It's absolutely devastating this period business. I'd quite forgotten just how destabilizing the whole thing of being a woman is.'

When Vivien crept back to her bed Patrick was already asleep and snoring. She was touched and thought how very like a married couple they had in fact become, because she didn't wake him up for the business interrupted by Deborah's catastrophe.

CHAPTER FOURTEEN

Deborah's strictures on Orlando's maintenance were as inconvenient to the round-the-clock Cora as is the Geneva Convention to the security forces of repressive states. By Day Two she was no longer even conscious of breaking rules, although she prudently kept an illicit tube of teething relief gel hidden in her anorak pocket and she did grind up some of the African root supplied by Deborah for the same purpose. Cora hoped that Orlando would only have a subliminal memory of the audio-masticatory joys of potato crisps, the comfort of milked-down sugary tea. She felt herself to be as much a victim as a tyrant. While the buggy wheels churned through old fish and chip wrappings and the park pigeons flocked to the crisps Orlando cast overboard, she recited lists of the various types of coal and their properties to herself, just as political prisoners survive spells of solitary by learning difficult languages.

Cora's strategy was one of so thoroughly exhausting Orlando that when the time came for his long sleep he would capitulate to his cot just as he had done for her on Day One. But on Day Two this strategy failed. At the appointed hour on Saturday evening Orlando got up a second wind and began a Great Refusal. While Deborah was being led around Bloomingdale's children's department by Sophie Weiss, a desperately dispirited Cora was battling with an Orlando whose red and howling face reared back at the very sight of his specially imported breast-shaped bottle. Cora's own cup of coffee went cold and she began to feel a weirdly melancholic longing for a mother herself, not the mother she could hardly remember, just some other adult against whom she could regress. But there was to be no slackening of the invisible chain between her and Orlando, no Deborah coming home to take over, not even Gloria, for she had not responded to Cora's knocks on her door.

Eventually Cora decided on the adulterous expedient of taking Orlando into her own bed. In her milk-stained tracksuit she lay down beside him and like a broncobuster gripped him round his middle until he stopped bucking the mattress with his head. At last he sighed and closed his eyes, and soon his little body was vibrating to the sound of disproportionately loud snores. But as soon as Cora began to disentangle herself from him, removing the foot that was lodged against her throat, he jerked to attention and was off again with a siren cry. Another refused bottle, another change of nappy later and Cora took the only recourse left to her. She carried a triumphantly silenced Orlando down-stairs, wrapped him up in his lambskin fleece and put him into Deborah's pre-war pram. She wheeled it out of the conservatory at the back of the house to bump it down the front steps and out into the street. Although some unwritten law said that babies should not go out at night, Deborah had never thought of expressly forbidding Cora to take Orlando out for jaunts in the dark. The springs of the pram creaked ominously as Cora pushed it forward but from deep within it Orlando gave out a raffish gurgle.

Cora had seldom been out alone at night and she was not, technically speaking, alone now. But even from within the purdah of Deborah's tall and solid house, the special sounds of Saturday night in that part of the city were audible. The thud-thud of household music systems gear-ing up for parties, the slow hum of pleasure traffic as immaculately groomed cars did their local exercises. Such cars, the mobile salons of the black working class, now cruised along the pavement beside Cora. Their drivers

133

stopped as they drew parallel with motoring acquaintances, as oblivious of the cortèges behind them as their
demurely glamorous female passengers seemed of them.

In the high street the greengrocer's, the dry cleaner's, the
chemist's, the betting shop and Ahmed's were shut and
dark, but the snooker club, the mini cab office and the fish
and chip shop were lit up and busy. Knots of young men on
the pavement outside these premises grinned at the lady
with the pram, and someone commented that her vehicle
need oiling. But the ribaldry was casual and fleeting, and
Orlando's just visible eyes were shut. It was as though the
pram in front of Cora were a charmed barge aboard which
she could sail through the stormiest seas. She felt serene as
she wheeled it forth and her recovery from the despair of
the previous hours was marked by pangs of hunger. She
pushed Orlando into the fish and chip shop and bought a
large bag of chips from a grey-faced man who had not seen
the sun of his native Cyprus for many years. Resolutely,
she elbowed her way to the salt and vinegar counter and
the other customers stood aside as she steered the pram
back out of the shop with one hand. She thought of turning
back to eat her chips at home but since they were already
staining the pram coverlet she paused to eat them outside
the butcher's shop. The saturated chips seemed puzzlingly
delicious, for hadn't Jesus been tormented by the vinegar-
soaked sponge tendered to him on a spear by the Roman
soldiers? Never mind, Cora did not dwell on this thought.
Instead she smiled at the enforced jollity of the slogans on
the butcher's window: you don't have to be crazy to work
here but it helps.

Orlando was now conclusively asleep but for her own
enjoyment Cora decided to do the full circuit, right to the
end of the high street, around the Fernwood Estate, which
on its other side bordered with Rochdale Gardens, and up
Chapel Grove from its other end. She was nearing the end
of the high street when a familiar figure, made even taller

134

by a turret-shaped yellow beret, emerged from the door-way of the Exodus Club.

'Where you taking that baby?'

Cora jumped out of her reverie to face Makeda's Nim-rod. 'For a walk,' she said cheekily, 'it's the only way to get him off to sleep.'

'Go back home now. There's trouble at Fernwood. It's not safe. Go home.'

To insist on his point the mighty Nimrod grabbed hold of the pram and lifted it up so that it faced back down the way Cora had come. Then, as more men came out of the club, he sauntered off across the street. Sighing, Cora trundled homewards. The lights were still on in the snooker hall and the mini-cab office, but the fish and chip shop had shut prematurely and the pavement population had melted away. She was back on Chapel Grove, within six houses of Deborah's house, when a voice rang out:

> 'And she wheeled her wheelbarrow,
> Through streets broad and narrow,
> Crying cockles and mussels,
> Crying cockles and mussels, alive, alive oh.'

Cora did not look behind to confirm her Guardian Angel's identity. A veritable rocket powered her and the pram up the front steps and into the house, a job normally comparable with the driving of Hannibal's elephants over the Alps. She gasped as she shut the door and immediately bolted it. But despite having been shunted down to the very bottom of the pram, Orlando was still sound asleep. Still, it seemed best now to keep him in her own bed for the night, and before lying down beside him she found the Luger and put it on her bedside table.

An hour or so later Cora was awakened by sounds of shouting and running. She coralled the perimeter of the bed with pillows and crept over to the window. Directly across from her she saw that the skips outside the builder's yard were in flames. Groups of teenagers, mainly male and black, were scurrying down the middle of the road with scarves tied cowboy-style across the lower part of their faces, while below Cora's window, in the front garden, some of them were crouching behind the hedge. Suddenly, they shot back out the gate and soon a crowd of about fifteen were bumping Deborah's Volvo into the middle of the road, so that it formed a T-shaped barricade with the blazing skips.

Cora rubbed her eyes and raised the window. Her room filled with the smell of burning rubber and she shut it again quickly. Just then a phalanx of policemen in black riot helmets charged down Chapel Grove. As the Volvo burst into flames its incinerators fanned out and ran like billy-o in the direction of the high street. Cora put on her shoes, grabbed the gun and crept downstairs. When she heard voices in the back garden she went to bolt the conservatory door and she was back in the main hallway, deliriously debating about what if anything she could do about Deborah's car, when Gloria's door opened behind her and the old lady herself appeared.

Bearing before her Gordon's leather-covered torch and dressed in a Guinevere-style green velour lounger, Gloria pranced by the pram like Liberty weaving her way through the barricades. She was followed by two men, Leander, the womb-knitter's son, and a middle-aged white, who was immediately recognizable to Cora as none other than the tuneful watcher-man. 'Hah!' she wanted to cry out, 'so you got yourself singed serenading me did you?'

Instead she found herself following the procession into the kitchen where, while Leander headed for the telephone, watcher-man resuscitated the range fire in best boy scout fashion. He shovelled in coal and called out, 'Any sign of some nosh Glo? There's nothing like a riot for whetting one's appetite.'

Gloria took one look in Deborah's fridge and turned on her heel. With a few minutes she had returned from her own larder with half a pound of best back rashers, a box of eggs and two cans of baked beans.

'Jolly good,' said the watcher-man, rubbing his hands. When Leander had finished his telephone conversation Gloria reintroduced him to Cora. But she seemed to think an introduction superfluous in the case of watcher-man and imperiously demanded a suitable pan for the beans. Without saying anything, Cora found Gloria the necessaries. Meanwhile Leander sat on the fertility seat and began to clean his glasses, and watcher-man turned on the radio. As he listened to the news bulletin he wore an expression of benign disdain.

'The Chapel Grove area of London has been sealed off because of the public disturbance that broke out earlier this evening in the Fernwood Estate. The trouble started just after nine p.m. as police broke into a flat believed to contain stolen goods. So far fifty arrests have been made and two policemen have been injured. At St Phillip's Hospital. . . .'

He turned off the radio and sighed, 'Nothing new. We'll get more news at midnight.' Where had he listened to the last bulletin, Cora wondered? She had her back to him most of the time as she basted the frying eggs and stirred the beans, and no one seemed to have noticed her gun, which she had slipped into the flour bin. Gloria was briskly setting the table, for four people even though she herself rarely ate anything more substantial than cream cheese on slimming crackers, and Cora had not indicated that she was hungry. Watcher-man came down Cora's end of the kitchen to bring the warmed-up plates to the table.

'You don't recognize me, do you Cora?'

'Of course I do.' Cora tried to sound indignant but in truth she was baffled by the assumption in his lighthearted, bantering voice that she should have recognized him in some congenial capacity. She was angered by his utterly unembarrassed presence in her employer's sacred kitchen and, supposing that he took his licence from Gloria, she looked crossly over at her. But the old lady looked boldly back at her and stuck her tongue out. Observing this, watcher-man moved closer to Cora and put one of his arms around her shoulders. He smiled into her face as he introduced himself: 'Frank Watson. I used to give you excellent tips for your excellent ham sandwiches.'

Cora wriggled away from his embrace and refused the hand he offered. Instead, she beckoned Gloria to the food and sat herself down at the table, where Leander was already seated. She crammed her mouth with food so as to buy time. Frank Watson simply sighed and placed himself beside Gloria, who was soon nursing a large whisky siphoned off from the bottle Jasmine had confiscated from her flat after the last cleaning raid.

'It's classic, Glo,' he said, giving Cora a reproachful look, 'there I was, unobtrusively patronizing this young woman's uncle's establishment, and giving her good tips, and she doesn't even remember me?'

'Oh yes,' Cora shouted out with her mouth full. She did now recall a more tanned version of her watcher-man, whom Uncle Willy had dubbed 'one of nature's gentlemen', whatever that was supposed to mean, and who was always looking for change for the pub's phone. 'What are you doing here? Why are you always hanging around here?'

Gloria laughed a loud and mocking laugh. 'He used to live here,' she said as she stubbed her cigarette into the bowl containing Orlando's teething potion, 'until superbitch slung him out.'

'Now now Glo. With hindsight it becomes possible to view Deborah's behaviour in a more charitable light.'

But now Leander, who had scarcely uttered a word since commencing his supper, pointed up at the ceiling and then Cora herself heard Orlando's wailing. 'Excuse me,' she said stiffly, for the first time ever welcoming Orlando's disruptive sense of timing.

He was very wet and so was the almost perfect circle drawn by his rotating body on Cora's bed. She took him

138

into the nursery and spent an inordinately long time changing him. Right, she thought to herself, two coincidences were just credible. This Frank Watson had been one of the journalists in Rathbwee after the besieging of Raging Bull and he was the same Frank whose belongings were still in the attic, whose books had been in Cora's bedroom and whose name was frequently coupled with Gordon's when Deborah railed against the deficiencies of menkind. But this coincidence did not explain what he was doing in the house at that hour. Still, Cora was comforted by her growing hope that whatever was going on had nothing much to do with her own immediate past, although it clearly had something to do with her present role at Chapel Grove. Orlando raised his head from Cora's shoulder as she walked into the kitchen, swaying his body in Frank's direction and falling happily into his embrace. Cora frowned.

'Sit down,' said Gloria, patting the chair beside her, 'that's what he's come for, to see his own babby.' Frank held Orlando up and invited Cora to inspect him closely. 'It's an open secret. Just look at him.'

'Just look at him,' Gloria repeated, 'he came at eight months and eight pounds.' She seemed indifferent to the fact that she was disowning Orlando as her own flesh and blood, and Orlando had set about acknowledging his newly designated father by pulling off his spectacles. But Cora couldn't see much of a resemblance between the babbling baby and the very tall man. Weakly, she sat down on the chair beside Gloria and the old lady offered her a cigarette.

'No thank you,' she said primly, 'you know I don't smoke.' Gloria then offered one to Leander and waved the packet at Frank, but he shook his head at her. 'We don't want Orlando to be a passive smoker, do we?'

'Good on you,' said Gloria as she lit up regardless, 'I'm too old to change.'

Cora watched helplessly as Frank Watson looked into

Orlando's face and said softly, 'Hallo little chap, I'm your Dad.' Then she rose again and fetched the milk, wordlessly presenting it to Frank and kneeling down beside his chair as he inserted the bottle into Orlando's mouth.

'Glo here's kept me informed. She's always had a soft spot for me.' Gloria confirmed this with a smile and proceeded to lace Leander's tea with whisky.

'But what about Gordon?' Cora whispered, 'why was nothing said to me?'

Gloria snorted from her snug at the supper table. 'He know's bloody well what's been going on, and he's got another brat to be going on with. That's the whole foolishness of big Deborah's plan. She thought Frank here was putting it about too much to be Daddy, but Gordon was the one to watch . . . if she'd cared to ask my opinion.'

Frank was more jovial as he took up Gloria's refrain. 'Granny Arkworth had the kindness to invite me round when Deborah was away so that I could become acquainted with my own son. But we didn't arrange the riot, did we Glo?'

Cora pursed her lips. 'I don't really understand any of this, or what you're on about. So if you don't mind I'll wait until Deborah comes home before I try to see what's right or wrong in what you're telling me.'

'Very proper, very proper. Why should you comprehend my relationship with this infant's mother?' Frank's tone was mocking, even, Cora dared to think, flirtatious, and Orlando withdrew from his half-empty bottle to beam up at him in complicity. Soon after Frank had hoisted him up on his shoulder, knocking his glasses sideways in the process but successfully inducing several large burps, Orlando went off to sleep again. Cora made no protest when Frank took him off upstairs to his cot. He did seem to know his way round the house and Cora was too dog-tired to exert her authority as Deborah's feeble vicar on Earth. Besides, by now the kitchen scene had a bizarre but beguiling cosiness to it. Facing her portable bar kit and the dirty supper dishes, Gloria looked like the Mad Hatter presiding over his tea party, with Leander, now asleep with his face over his folded arms, as the reluctant dormouse. But Deborah's vegetarian kitchen, already defiled by the fry-up, also began to smell strongly of Gloria's French cigarettes and so some of Cora's anxious energy returned. She felt like a child who has been bullied into playing some forbidden game by older children. With her eyes streaming in the smoke, she walked to the kitchen front window and peered outside. By now Deborah's car was a burnt-out shell. It looked like one of the foreboding animal carcasses that litter the deserts across which wagons trail in westerns.

'She had loads of documents in there I'm sure,' she said sadly, 'but I couldn't do anything really.'

'No,' the returned Frank tried to reassure her, 'it happened very quickly. I was watching from Glo's.'

'In any case, it's probably well insured, and if it's that bloody couvade rubbish she had in there, good riddance to bad rubbish I say. That was the last straw to my way of thinking, rustling up total strangers to play daddies with . . . men aren't like snails you dump in buckets of bran to make sweet.'

'Now now Glo, that's enough. Can't you see that little Cora here is very tired and ought to be sent to bed.' But Gloria carried on muttering furiously to herself until Leander raised his head to look at her with some resentment. He had been passing the house when the police charged down Chapel Grove and had ducked round the back to rap on Gloria's window, just as he used to before Cora was on hand to accept the woolly womb deliveries. Frank said he would show Leander up to the spare room at the very top of the house but he was unspecific about where he proposed to lay his own head down. When he returned, he gathered up the egg-smeared plates, telling Cora as he dumped them in the sink that 'we Englishmen make very good wives'. When insisting, for the third time, that she should retire, he even mustered the authority of her Uncle Willy, whom he had re-encountered on a fishing holiday in Rathbwee and who had allegedly instructed him to 'keep an eye' on his niece in London. So with Frank's cheeky, somewhat ironic solicitude still ringing in her ears, Cora bowed out of the kitchen.

She fell asleep in a bed that smelled of baby urine, which Deborah would almost certainly have insisted was good for her skin, and woke up next morning to find that both Frank and Leander had left as discreetly as they had arrived. By the time Deborah rang up Orlando was in the kitchen creating an early Jackson Pollock with his porridge, while five photographers were kneeling in adoration around the Volvo in the street outside.

CHAPTER FIFTEEN

When Cora heard the diesel sound of Deborah's taxi drawing up she wiped Orlando's nose and stood on the porch steps to welcome the mistress home. It was a clean, calm morning and the kitchen was fragrant with riot-trampled wallflowers salvaged from the front garden.

The riot's aftermath was curiously cheerful. It had evoked something like a Blitz spirit among Deborah's neighbours, most of whom had been only marginally affected by it materially, and some of whom even took an embarrassed pride in their area's sudden notoriety. Local shopkeepers, including the articulate Ahmed, had become minor celebrities as a result of their appearances on television and flocks of people gathered spontaneously in the high street to feed on conflicting rumours about the government's response.

The optimists said that the Fernwood Estate was going to be demolished, that in its place a new urban village set in a landscaped public garden was to be built, to be opened by the Queen, Princess Di, or her husband, the Pope, or Stevie Wonder. The pessimists said that Fernwood was going to be hedged in by an electrified fence and its inhabitants bound by a police-enforced curfew. But most people, victims, rioters and riot-victims, knew that there was still plenty of dry tinder about in the form of depression, deprivation and discrimination for certain forms of police action to re-kindle at any time. Even so, individual refinements on the specific catalyst of Saturday night's contribution to modern British history abounded.

'It's the police,' said Jasmine, whose perspective was, depending on her listener, distorted or enlightened by the injuries sustained by her eldest son as he became caught up in the retreat down Chapel Grove.

'It's Babylon burning,' said Makeda, who Cora found grappling with the application forms for a nursing job in Zimbabwe. 'It's because Henry Ashe got stopped and searched on his way back from the chip shop with his kids' supper,' said Nimrod, always less poetic than his consort.

'It's white ultra-leftists stirring things up,' said the man who lived next door to Deborah, who was worried about the riot's impact on local house values.

'It's the IRA teaching the blacks to make petrol bombs,' said the greengrocer's battered wife, who did not know that you need no lessons to make petrol bombs and who would have been very flattered if she'd known that her version of the outside agitator line was being pursued by a bevy of imported detectives in the local police station.

Deborah was one of the pessimists but she did not voice her negative feelings. She filled in the forms enabling her to claim compensation for the car, which had been towed away by a police-authorized wrecker, and took Orlando out herself to tour the neighbourhood. (She returned, highly amused, to tell Cora about the curious old lady who had sung 'Lucky Jim' at him.) Cora had saved up choice details about Orlando's behaviour for Deborah. She told her how he'd eaten a whole avocado, how his latest tooth had been made manifest, and of how he'd waved at someone with both of his hands. This last delicacy had been a bit risky because that someone had been Frank Watson and Cora was uneasily waiting for him to reappear and square his fatherly ambitions with Deborah.

To a certain extent Deborah welcomed the exterior excitement generated by the riot because it gave her the space to cloak an inner turmoil arising from a new awareness of Gordon's other 'family' in San Francisco. An

144

old acquaintance from her truly married days, looked up in New York as a graceful way of leaving the lovey-dovey Patrick and Vivien time alone together, had mentioned the mother and child with whom he stayed on his regular visits to the West Coast. When Gordon had confided this child's existence to Deborah the mother was refusing him any place in the domestic picture. But this American friend's cosy references to the ménage suggested that Gordon had now managed to insert his spineless self in it, and that rocked Deborah's somewhat complacent ownership of her husband. It had been this disturbing realization as well as the 'London's Night of Terror' headlines in the American newspapers that had catapulted her home prematurely. Now she sat in her solar and revised her future.

Deborah decided to re-orientate herself purely as a writer-polemicist, to retire from her practical commitments to Nativities and quit the riotous inner city for a computer and a cottage in the country. There, Orlando could play without fear of traffic, lead poisoning and social contamination. Deborah was quite relieved that her couvade dossier had gone to Valhalla in the Volvo. The compassion for trees that had made her agonize about providing Cora with disposable nappies also meant that no copies of the couvade data existed. She was not in any case inclined to resuscitate a limping project that had lost its legs entirely with the evaporation of Gordon's viability as Orlando's father figure.

Deborah's next project concerned something fundamental, yes fundamental. She had decided to call her bowels book *Fundamentals* and her American collaborator was scheduled to visit London within a few months. Relevant ideas were leaping around Deborah's head. She expounded to Cora a vast Utopian scheme whereby the ancient organic relationship between town and country was to be reinvigorated by means of modern nightsoil carts.

'Human excrement is a precious thing,' she exclaimed as

145

she watched Cora scraping Orlando's bottom in the bathroom, 'and all that precious manure is presently destroyed by our sewage systems, so that farmers have to use nasty chemicals to make the soil fertile.'

Cora stuck Orlando's nappy together and washed her hands. She had not responded favourably to Deborah's proposal for a pilot scheme using Orlando's offerings in the back garden, and was disappointingly diffident about the prospect of a symbiotic relationship between the Fernwood Estate and some lush part of Buckinghamshire. She pointed out that Deborah's neighbours might object to the pilot scheme and suggested that the additives consumed by most people outside their particular house might adversely affect the manureal value of their waste. This last point was accepted by Deborah. 'I'll have to do more research on that one,' she said as she wandered back to her solar, and later she could be heard on the telephone quizzing Karen Zucker on the same topic.

Cora was as long-suffering as ever in the face of the new project but the first real casualty of Deborah's reorientation was to be Gloria. Her nearness now had no redeeming aspects with her unsolicited title as Orlando's grandmother in doubt along with her importance as the financial bedrock of the house. But Gloria did not appear for Deborah's denunciation. Like Marat, she'd gone underground since the riot. According to Ahmed, with whom Deborah had chatted while his new steel shutters were being erected, she had not 'patronized' his shop for several weeks. When she had not appeared above stairs for several days after Deborah's return Cora started to worry. But Deborah scorned Cora's concern and suggested that Gloria had probably had an unsuccessful new hairdo and was lying low until it wore off. That this explanation might not have been too uncharitably off the mark was indicated by the glorious smell of bacon and eggs – Gloria's new diet – wafting up from her basement every lunchtime. The smell offended Deborah's vegetarian nostrils and caused even more fulminations.

On Friday evening Vivien rang up to say that she was back at her flat, and that Patrick had gone on to his place. At last there was someone Cora could talk to about the internal events of the previous Saturday night. Also, since Deborah now talked of Patrick with possessive familiarity, as a great family friend, Cora was anxious to reclaim her brother for herself.

Rochdale Gardens had served as an arsenal during the riot. Empty milk and cider bottles no longer littered its doorsteps, for they had been taken off by Fernwood Estate residents who had returned there to stock up, like sleep-walkers haunting some familiar place. One house, until recently occupied by a pair of Scottish buskers, had been completely burnt out. As she stood outside this ruin Cora found herself within firing line of two television crews, one Swedish and one South African, the latter giving gleeful coverage to the English racial troubles. She hurried on until she was at Patrick's house but the door was locked. Makeda let her in and, unusually, relocked the door behind them.

'Patrick's not here,' she said, looking at Cora questioningly.

'Not here? Maybe he went to get us a takeaway dinner?'

Makeda said nothing. She beckoned Cora through the bead curtain leading to her kitchen, pushed aside the map of Zimbabwe on her table and poured her a cup of herbal tea.

'I don't think your brother's gone to get food. He went off with two guys in a yellow Cortina.' Makeda was not looking Cora in the eye. 'I didn't get a very good look at them, and Nimrod left by the back way because he thought they were coming for him. But they weren't local police. They took his toolkit with them and he asked me to ring you up. I was just about to when you called.'

147

The mug in Cora's hand slipped and she scalded her wrist. She sucked it, and looked hard at Makeda, while her legs shook under the table. If Makeda thought the men who'd gone off with Patrick were cops she was probably right. Like the other women at Rochdale Gardens, she had a fine eye for the subtle differences between the thugs hired by television rental companies to harass defaulters, the men who snooped on behalf of the Department of Health and Social Security, and all the other unwelcome but regular visitors to the street. Makeda was apologetically certain that Patrick's escorts had been policemen, not realising that at one level her conviction reassured Cora. With thoughts of her brother's self-appointed mission in New York on her mind, she had plenty of vague but equally sinister candidates to contemplate.

They went together to Patrick's big room which, despite Makeda's preliminary efforts, was still in considerable disarray, with gaping, half-disgorged drawers and the contents of an upturned waste-paper basket upended over the bed.

'Thank God he's so careful,' said Cora, noticing the absence of his smoking paraphernalia, and Makeda nodded. But then Cora glanced at the empty wall over the fireplace and her hand went over her mouth.

'Don't worry. We've got the gun in the yard. Nimrod borrowed it on Saturday night. But he's put it away somewhere safe.' Cora smiled in gratitude and told Makeda she'd be back to clean up the room herself. Then she ran all the way home.

'Oh there you are,' was Deborah's greeting, 'they've just rung from the police station.'

'What did they say?'

'He's helping them with some enquiries.'

'What enquiries?'

'How should I know?' Deborah's tone was casual as she shifted Orlando to her other hip, 'they don't have to charge him with anything under the Prevention of Terrorism Act.

It's probably some ridiculous mistake. Anyhow, I've rung Vivien and she'll take you down there.'

Cora muttered angrily to herself and stormed into the kitchen, where she began to fling food into a plastic carrier bag.

'Now don't be silly. Calm down and wait for Viv. Then you can go down and find out what it's all about.'

Cora looked at Deborah resentfully. She was so sincerely sure that it had been some 'ghastly mistake' because the police only said 'good morning' or gave directions to the like of Deborah Lieberman. She never flinched when prison vans flanked by shrieking police cars passed her on the high street on their way to court, and policemen never gave her a second glance. If they did, she only had to speak to put them in their place. But at least Vivien knew more. She had voluntarily joined the guilty in her days as a political activist. Cora slid into her car and allowed herself to be driven at an illegal speed to the local police station.

'I've got in touch with a lawyer, an old friend actually, and although Patrick can't see one under the PTA, he might be useful.'

'Good,' Cora said flatly. But when Vivien began to get out of the car with her she said as politely as she could that she'd prefer to go in alone.

'No way. You ought to have someone with you and Patrick's important to me too you know.' Then Cora noticed that they'd parked behind a yellow Cortina, and she made no further objections.

The reception area in the police station was crowded out by two queues of people, the majority of whom had filed behind a sign advertising 'General Riot Damage Enquiries'. Cora and Vivien joined the other, shorter queue and soon found themselves before a young policeman with rolled-up shirt sleeves who could not disguise his preoccupation with the half-eaten cheese sandwich lying on the counter beside his ledger.

'Well ladies, what can we do for you?' he asked with a flourish of his flaccid sandwich.

'I'd like to find out what's happening to my brother, Patrick Mangan, please,' Cora said in a small, absurdly deferential voice. She felt herself to be in a dream where she wanted to shout but could only come out with barely audible squeaks.

'What's the name again?' the policeman dared to take another bite of his sandwich.

'Patrick Mangan, Patrick Joseph Mangan.'

'Ah,' he took a close look at another ledger. 'Mrs Mangan?'

Cora said nothing but Vivien butted in. 'And Vivien Lieberman, a family friend. We'd like to see him.' To the fury of the two men behind Cora and Vivien in the queue, there to register a recently stolen car, the policeman then disappeared. While he was gone Cora stared at the posters on the walls around them, posters advising people on neighbourhood crime-prevention schemes and touching portraits of missing children, complete with details of the clothes they had last been seen in. On the way to the police station Vivien had talked defiantly about 'racist pigs', hoping, no doubt, to reassure Cora that she was equally convinced of Patrick's innocence. But looking at these posters, and at the array of miscellaneous petitioners gathered around them on that evening, Cora could not believe that there would ever be a time when the police would be redundant. The sheer regulative pressure of life in this vast city made them a necessary evil, even if Patrick had somehow got swept up by the broom and most of the people in the dustpan with him were only there on account of the colour of their skin.

The impatient men behind Cora and Vivien began clapping when the cheese-sandwich-eater finally emerged from a door at the side of the glass-fronted reception desk.

He asked the 'ladies' to follow him, leading them down a series of corridors and into a small room containing a table and two chairs.

'Wait here ladies please. Detective-Constable White will be with you shortly. He's tied up just at the moment.'

'Tied up?' said Vivien, 'So he's into bondage is he?' But the reception policeman didn't hear this and Cora was glad. She sat down and in the process her carrier bag fell open to fill the room with the smell of spring onions. 'Oh Cora my love aren't you just typical, bringing food for all contingencies.'

Vivien did not know that Cora's foresight was not a woman's kneejerk response to crisis but a gesture that connected Patrick's incarceration with her Rathbwee past and what she had involved him with as a result of losing that parcel. But Vivien's 'my love' lingered on in Cora's mind as a reminder of the postcard she'd received from her brother that very morning. Unusually, he'd signed off, 'love Patrick'. Now why would her otherwise unsentimental brother have done that unless words like 'love' were being extracted from him by someone else?

Detective-Constable White finally managed to disentangle himself. He wore a pale blue suit and he had a little Sandhurst-style moustache. Just to show how unimpressed she was, Vivien lit a cigarette, even though no ashtrays were visible. For once Cora wished that she, too, could smoke without spluttering and making a terrible fool of herself. She repeated their request.

'I'm afraid that's not possible Mrs Mangan.'

'Why?' said Vivien.

He looked at Cora again and said, 'Because he's not with us any longer. Mr Mangan has been taken to Paddington Green, which, as you may or may not know, is a rather more secure place than this. He will be held there until we are satisfied with our enquiries.'

'What enquiries?' Cora's brimming eyes were focused on the smelly carrier bag.

'I'm afraid that's not for me to say. But he is reasonably comfortable and if you leave us with details of where you can be contacted, we'll pass them on to Paddington Green.'

Vivien, whose Deborah-voice had now ripened, intervened again.

'Would you be so kind,' she said with lofty sarcasm, 'as to inform Mr Mangan of our visit. Also, perhaps you could pass on these cigarettes.'

Vivien handed over a carton of duty-free cigarettes and a fistful of booklets of matches.

'Where did these come from?' Detective-Constable White asked, holding up one of the Biltmore match booklets.

'Where it says, I thought you guys were supposed to be literate these days.' Then Vivien put her hands on Cora's shoulders and gently raised her to her feet. The detective lit himself a cigarette from one of the Biltmore booklets and personally escorted them back out to the reception desk.

'Come on Vivien,' Cora said quietly. She was now grateful for her presence but worried about Vivien's talent for getting people's backs up. 'There's nothing more we can do here.'

'This little lady's got sense,' Detective-Constable White leered at Vivien as he opened the main door for them.

'Oh don't be such a wet Cora,' Vivien said when they reached her car. 'It might be important.'

'What might be important?'

'Those matches, corroborating where he was during the riot. They've lifted Paddies from all over town because of that bomb factory they think they've found on the Fernwood Estate.'

'Oh maybe you're right then.' But Cora's acceptance of Vivien's *sang froid* was grudging. On the way home Vivien stopped the car because her lawyer friend always went to bed early and she wanted to tell him about the meeting. She left the car headlights on so that she could see the dial on the phone. In a daze Cora watched Vivien's animated figure in the phone box. She remembered Patrick telling her to ring him at the Crown if she ever needed to get hold of him in a hurry, something she'd actually done only once, on her first day with Orlando when he looked as if he were dying from the attack of wind that resulted from a bottle of Deborah's expressed milk. She remembered her hopes and anxieties on the boat to England, and the old man who had been sitting opposite her on the train at Holyhead. The train was stationary for a long time and he had kept saying, 'They're just checking their computer now, the police computer, that's what's holding us all up.'

'Is that so?' a more sociable woman passenger had said. 'It's a wonder then that they don't catch them oftener.'

'Ah but you see,' the old man carried on with a self-satisfied tug of his unlit pipe, 'it's only the young fellahs with the beards and the rucksacks they put into it. They don't bother with the likes of me. Sure I could be the Divil himself and no one would be the wiser.'

'Oh now,' his listener humoured him, 'don't be telling us you're really who they're after.' Then the old man had given her a look of superior mysteriousness and Cora had shifted again and slid under her anorak.

As soon as Vivien was back in the car with her seatbelt fastened, Cora's rapid rewind of the immediate past stopped and she unlocked hers. 'I'd like to make a call as well,' she mumbled as she peered at a piece of paper. Vivien passed her a torch and leaned over her as she deciphered Frank Watson's number. In his capacity as the godfather appointed by her uncle Willy, Frank had told her to ring him up if she ever felt a need of his help.

'Frank Watson!' Vivien exclaimed. 'That's Frank's number. You're not involved with him are you?'

Cora lay back in her seat and groaned.

'Just about every female in town's got Frank's number. That's why Debbo threw him out. He's probably Orlando's Dad you know, if you could call him that since, as she tells us so often, fatherhood is a socially constructed status.'

153

'So you know all about him,' was all Cora could say.

'Sure. He used to have your room, and Gloria's never forgiven my sister for breaking with him. But don't let me stop you from ringing him. He does know a bit about this sort of thing.' Vivien leaned over Cora's lap to open her door, and kept the headlights beamed on the phone box. But to Cora's relief only an answering machine responded to the number she dialled, and she put the phone down without leaving a message.

Deborah smelled of perfume and she beamed most incongruously at the war widows when they returned to Chapel Grove.

'We've saved you supper,' she announced jovially, 'Frank's just upstairs putting Orlando to bed.'

'Frank Watson?' Vivien gave Cora a knowing grin, but she scuttled off to hang up her jacket without making eye contact with either of the sisters.

'Yes, my Frank. He's been here for the past while and we've been having a little pow-wow, sorting some things out.'

'Oh yeah, your Frank. That sounds very civilized. Have you decided to give our Orlando a double oedipus complex then?'

Deborah ignored Vivien. She took Cora's stinking carrier bag and in a loud confident voice told her that Frank was sure there was nothing to worry about: 'They do this sort of thing regularly. It's routine, just a precaution in case he unwittingly knows someone, or something, they're after. Frank says they'll probably release him after a couple of days without charging him, unless, of course, he was carrying anything.'

'No. He's always very careful about that, and they took him off in his new suit.'

Deborah nodded her satisfaction.

'But if he does have any substances on him, he can always say he's a Nativities birthmate, can't he Debbo? That

154

would be the perfect excuse.'

Deborah did not look gratified by Vivien's suggestion and she ignored her sister until Frank came downstairs. He embraced Viven and winked at Cora, who managed a weak smile back. But when a steaming plate of macaroni cheese was put in front of her she rose and said that she didn't feel hungry. Vivien looked put out by this announcement because she herself had a great appetite in spite of Patrick's trouble and she did not want to appear less concerned than Cora. But Frank said that she should go to bed and Deborah made her a cup of Valerian-flavoured tea: 'You've got to look after yourself Cora. We don't want you in bad condition for those exams.'

Cora raised her duvet to find a floury Luger pistol wrapped in a tea towel. A note from Frank accompanied it: 'Found this when I was making the roux. Don't you think Orlando's a little young for such toys?'

CHAPTER SIXTEEN

Nothing about the examination hall surprised Cora, although the *déjà vu* sensation she had upon entering it probably said more about the uniformity of examination centres than it did about the prophetic accuracy of her recent anxiety dreams. It was a dreary old schoolhall with high church-like windows, used only for keep fit classes, jumble sales and adult examinations since a new school had been built on the Fernwood Estate. It smelled of floor polish and sweat, and even on a tolerably mild day in June it was cold. Most of the examinees, including Cora, kept jackets and cardigans on as they twiddled the little pieces of card on which their examination numbers were written and waited for the starter's orders.

The invigilator shuffled between the desks in carpet slippers, distributing bright pink examination papers. Half an hour in, a man in a bloated anorak in front of Cora raised his hand to summon the invigilator for another answer book; behind Cora another man swore aloud; and the woman with the skinny blonde plait to her right groaned. It was always bad for morale when someone asked for more paper so early, but maybe the anorak-man had big handwriting? Some people did when they were nervous. At any rate, soon Cora had also broken ranks and the invigilator, wearing an unnecessarily grave and severe expression throughout, came down from her desk at the top of the hall with another answer book. When there were only about ten minutes left, Cora read back through her answer books, neatened her diagrams with the fine red pen Frank had given her, and sat with her arms folded while her destiny was taken away.

This kind of lonely meritocratic hurdling suited Cora. You didn't need a sparkling personality to do well in examinations and success with one led to another, and then more. During the break between papers Cora did not mingle with the other candidates, not wishing to learn of some misinterpretation of a question or to share in the general anxiety about the afternoon session. She sat alone in a nearby car park and stained her cheese sandwiches with ink.

'You need your eyes testing, you blind bat! You've just stared right through me.' Cora jumped as she was accosted by Vivien. 'I said I'd come and collect you. How was it? Or don't you want to talk about it?'

Cora squinted into the golden light of the late afternoon and shook her head, and so Vivien didn't push her.

'Debbo and Frank went to the hypermarket this morning and they're going to cook us a nice meal tonight.'

'That's nice,' said Cora, who was shivering while Vivien was comfortable in shorts and a T-shirt. 'That's nice, but I still don't really understand how they've been able to make everything so hunky-dory so. . . .'

'Oh you will when you're older. Deborah's just tired and Frank's made a packet. She can't make that kind of money from Nativities. It's not in her nature anyhow, and she's got to the stage where she fancies winter holidays in the sun and that.'

'But it can't be that easy,' Cora insisted. As she was being led to the car park she was wishing she had the courage to ask if her brother had been murmuring about winter holidays in the sun. But Cora didn't want to offend Vivien with questions that cast doubts on Patrick's integrity, and she acquiesced with a wave of a limp wrist when Vivien suggested a quick drink at the Crown.

Theresa had just opened the bar up. The tobacco-stained

curtains were flapping in the warm breeze and for once the juke box was silent. It was too early for any of the regulars, although Vivien was about to acquire such status on account of many recent visits to Patrick's club.

'Hallo girls,' Theresa said when she'd finished reloading the cigarette machine, 'what can I get for ye today?'

Vivien asked for two halves of lager with lime. Even when seated her tanned thighs did not spread out much. She told Cora that she'd visited Rochdale Gardens earlier in the day and passed a bundle of letters over to her with an air of scrupulous disregard. Cora began to sift them on her lap, setting one little pile aside on the table. Vivien stretched out an arm and picked up one of these letters.

'Who's the lucky woman then?'

Cora frowned

'Who is Mrs P.J. Mangan?'

'A friend of Makeda's. She's South African and she works at the same hospital. Makeda usually takes these letters in to her. Patrick hardly knows her really.'

'A political marriage of convenience?' Vivien sounded very relieved. 'That was noble of him.'

Cora shrugged. 'Not really. It doesn't cost him anything. Anyhow, she's thinking about a divorce now because she's involved with an English bloke she wants to marry.'

Theresa then did her female customers the honour of carrying over their drinks. 'No news I suppose?'

'No,' said Vivien, 'nothing.'

'Ah well, I'm sure it will be all right soon. He never had any time for them at all. I mean he'd put a few bob in the prisoners' fund from time to time, but that was the size of it.' Vivien smiled gratefuly, but Cora could not be so easily reassured. No one, least of all his women's support caucus at the Crown, really knew what Patrick might have been up to.

'Have you seen Enda about?' Cora asked Theresa sharply.

'No, not a sight nor sound of him, and I can tell you

158

there's a fair few looking for him.' But then, as the first of her real regulars sloped in, Theresa scurried back behind the bar.

'Enda?' Vivien asked.

'The plasterer who worked on Gloria's place. Patrick used to say he had connections.'

'Oh,' Vivien giggled, 'for a moment I thought it was another wife.'

Cora smiled weakly at her.

'You know,' Vivien continued, 'I did wonder why that detective kept calling you Mrs Mangan. They must have just assumed you were the missus.'

'I suppose so.'

'You suppose so, you sly thing. What else are you keeping from me?'

'Nothing, honestly, nothing.' This was not true and Cora felt a little guilty about that because she was very grateful for Vivien's wholehearted support, which protected her from any doubts being entertained by Deborah on the subject of her nanny's respectability. Just as Cora had been able to push her abortion to one side, so she had suspended her worry about Patrick while she concentrated on the exam. But now she was busy forgetting about the exam and so Vivien expected her to be more forthcoming about Patrick, who had been in custody for four days. Cora had done her best to feed Vivien's hunger for news of him by telling her as much as she could remember about the bits of childhood she'd shared with her brother. She had even told Vivien about her abortion, though not the identity of the man who'd caused it. But there were things Cora still felt she had a responsibility to keep quiet about because, despite the strength of the claim Vivien had staked on him, Cora did not yet know for certain that Patrick appreciated it.

Since Frank had negotiated his way back into her and Orlando's life, on terms that had yet to be made public although a vasectomy was almost certainly among them, Deborah had embarked on an orgy of domesticity. She made herself some new clothes and a quilt for Orlando, and did a great deal of cooking. When Gloria had been seen setting off with her shopping bags on the afternoon of Cora's second examination, Deborah immediately phoned Jasmine, who had been unable to gain access to the basement flat on the previous week. But about a quarter of an hour after she'd first ventured down there Jasmine came running back upstairs. She stood on the threshold of the big kitchen, peeled off her rubber gloves and flung them like gauntlets at the table where Deborah was rolling out the pastry for an asparagus quiche.

'That's it. That is it. I've had enough.'

'Jasmine?' Deborah looked concerned but not alarmed. She expected to learn of the latest pest to have found sanctuary in her mother-in-law's flat.

'I've had enough of that disgusting old witch and her filthy place. I've had it up to here,' Jasmine pointed at her ears, 'with all her filth and rubbish and I can't take no more.'

Deborah sighed and downed her rolling pin. 'What's wrong now?'

'She's got a man in that bed of hers.'

'A man?'

'A dead man, a stinking rotten corpse.'

Frank came down from the nursery to find out what Jasmine had been shouting about. He and Deborah immediately went down Gloria's rickety steps to investigate for themselves, leaving Jasmine to hold on to Orlando and keep a look-out against the old lady's sudden return.

On all the available surfaces in Gloria's bedroom there were plates of untouched fried food: congealed baked beans, plastic-looking fried eggs, stiff chips, grey rashers of bacon and sausages around which a coating of white fat had dried. They looked like those sad dinners placed in some café windows as inadvertent black propaganda for

160

the wares obtainable inside. In the bed itself, face down-wards on a grimy pillow, was the body of a halfdressed elderly man. His sports jacket was hanging over the back of an armchair and a man's handkerchief had been placed over the bedside lamp so as to dull the light further.

'Good grief!' said Frank, 'who is it?' He turned off the lamp and pulled the curtains while Deborah gently turned the corpse's head to one side.

'It's that plasterer chap,' said Deborah. 'No wonder she's not been going out much lately. They must have had quite a little scene going for themselves down here.'

Frank rubbed his chin and said, only half-jokingly, 'You know I've always imagined that Glo might be done one day for harbouring stolen goods, but you don't think she's gone in for body-snatching do you?'

Deborah just snorted and redrew the curtains. In best beer hall waitress fashion she gathered up some of the plates of food, and as they marched grimly upstairs she began to give her orders. Deborah herself would ring the police, Gordon, and Gloria's doctor, in that order; Frank was to go out in search of Gloria and to bring her back without arousing her suspicions; and Jasmine was to stay with Orlando. But Deborah's command of the situation was disrupted by the return of Cora and Vivien. When Cora caught the drift of what Jasmine was saying she hurried off to the basement to confirm Enda's identity for herself. On the bedside table she found something that no one else had noticed, or would miss – a strapless gold watch inscribed at the back with the words P.J. Mangan, 3 March 1934. She slipped it into her pocket, drew the top sheet over Enda's face and went back upstairs to receive Deborah's revised orders.

'You go and find Gloria, Cora, and get her back here as fast as you can without letting on that anything's up.'

Cora charged off in the direction of the high street. How was it, she thought as she wandered deliriously in and out of all the shops, that her life never moved on in a measured way. Instead it took drastic, jerky leaps forward in a matter of days, just as Orlando was capable of staying the same weight for a month, only to gain a whole pound, several new teeth and some novel physical skill within one week. She was despairing of her mission until she passed the Topiary salon and saw Gloria inside, having her nails buffed by Samson. She hovered outside, away from the window, until Gloria emerged.

'Hallo, little student.' Gloria probably thought Cora was walking home from the examination centre. She smelled of the same perfume Deborah had taken to wearing recently, which disconcerted Cora, and from each of her freshly manicured hands were suspended string bags full of cans of baked beans and packets of sausages.

'Here,' said Cora, taking these paniers of cholesterol, 'let me take these home for you.'

'Oh that's very nice of you,' Gloria said fondly, 'but I wasn't thinking of going home just yet. It's such a nice evening I thought I'd take a stroll in the Park. Wouldn't you like to come with me?'

'No,' Cora could not avoid sounding firm, 'not today. We should go home now.' She transferred the string bags to one arm and linked the other with Gloria's. Slowly, they rounded the corner into Chapel Grove where, even from a distance, the spattering noise of the police radios in the cars drawing up outside the house was audible. Gloria stiffened suddenly and withdrew her arm.

'Police. What are they doing?'

'It's Enda. He's not well you know. He needs help.' Never in her whole life had Cora felt as treacherous as she did at that moment.

'I know,' the mascara began to run down Gloria's cheeks, 'he hasn't been eating properly for days now, no matter what I cook for him.'

A knot of curious neighbours and passers-by had now gathered on the street across from the house, watching the policemen coming in and going out from all angles, like ants scurrying around a flagstone. While one went in with a camera and tripod, another was drawing chalk lines on the garden path, and others emerged holding bags containing bits and pieces of 'evidence', like goldfish in plastic bags. Gloria remained rooted to the pavement. She stared impassively at all the comings and goings until Enda's body was brought out on a stretcher, his body draped with unintentional propriety by a green blanket. Then she let out a scream and rushed towards the house.

'You fat bitch, you've been spying on me,' she shouted at Deborah, who had stepped outside the front door.

'Please,' Cora pleaded with her, 'please don't upset yourself more.' With Frank's help she persuaded Gloria to go into the house while Enda's body was being placed in an ambulance. Ten minutes later Gloria came out again with Frank and her doctor. But before sitting in the doctor's car she took a long hard look at the ambulance, the doors of which had just been shut, and called out to the onlookers across the road, 'How do you get twenty-four Brits into a taxi then?' There was a silence until she answered her own defiant question, 'You put the foreman in first and the rest crawl up his arse.' Then Gloria laughed a loud and hopelessly vindictive laugh, and was driven away to the hospital.

One of the neighbours could be heard guffawing and Vivien could be seen grinning through the kitchen window. But Cora just looked down at her shoes in embarrassment and silence, and fingered her father's watch in her pocket. Inside the house she heard Deborah telling the most senior police officer that her mother-in-law had not been in her right mind for some time, that she and her husband had managed to keep her under control but that their absence had caused her to lapse in this dramatic way. 'What could we do? She's had no end of undesirable types in that place of hers in the past.' The police officer nodded sympathetically and assured Mrs Arkworth-Lieberman that no charges were likely to be pressed against such an eccentric and obviously ill old lady. Then Deborah turned to Jasmine and asked her to make tea for the remaining policemen.

'No way,' said Jasmine, picking up her bag and buttoning her jacket, 'I've got my principles. No way.'

But Cora 'was afraid' she couldn't do that either, so Deborah had to make the tea herself while Frank gave Orlando his bath.

Two hours later, while a tranquillized Gloria was sleeping in St Phillip's Hospital, Patrick Joseph Mangan was released from Paddington Green without charge. A jubilant Vivien went to bring him to Chapel Grove for a dinner delayed in his honour. Although Patrick's face was suspiciously puffy on one side he looked strangely dignified and formal in his wrinkled linen suit. Cheered on and frequently interrupted by Vivien, who pushed food in his direction like a farmer's wife feeding harvest workers, his own account of his ordeal was jokey and incomplete.

'Luckily,' he said between mouthfuls of Deborah's deluxe quiche, 'I wasn't carrying any illegal substances. I'd barely got home in fact, and had just come from the shops when the buggers turned up and frightened Makeda out of her wits.'

'It's ridiculous,' Deborah huffed, 'you know if they had found anything on you you could have said you'd been invited to a birth. Many of our clients use cannabis.'

'Really Debbo,' Vivien's voice was sarcastic, 'you mean you would have welcomed that kind of publicity.'

'Well, it's a jolly good thing they didn't find some charge to pin on you,' Frank intervened to stop the sisters from squabbling, 'but I must say it was most unfortunate that you'd mislaid your passport.'

Patrick winced and nodded his agreement at this comment.

'Yes,' Vivien dug him in the ribs, 'you silly chump. Imagine losing your passport on your way home from the airport. No wonder they beat you up! They probably thought it was the most outrageous alibi they'd ever heard, being on the Concorde and everything. Wasn't it lucky I happened to have some of those Biltmore matches, though I suppose they'd have let you go anyhow once Enda had been found.'

Cora's eyes narrowed at this exchange. Lost his passport indeed. Where had he posted it to, and who was now travelling under his name? But Patrick shot her a bold and brassy smile, and she gave in and smiled back at him. There were things that neither of them would ever know about each other.

'What kind of things did they ask you?' she asked him, still vaguely worried that she had unwittingly precipitated the whole business.

Patrick raised his hands and shrugged. 'Everything, and it was only after a few sessions that I realized it was Enda they were after.'

'Everything you can imagine,' Vivien broke in, 'where he shopped and where he drank, and who his friends were and when he'd last been to Ireland, everything.'

Patrick left it at that, and then Frank raised his glass to propose a toast to his return, to Gloria's recovery, which Deborah hoped might eventually result in her transfer to an old folks' home, and, last but not least, to Cora's success.

'How do you think it went, I haven't had a chance to ask you,' Frank turned to Cora. She answered him boldly, 'Well, I think.'

CHAPTER SEVENTEEN

Marie-Antoinette is said to have turned grey within a matter of days after the failure of the Flight to Varennes, a case, perhaps, of nature expressing drastic solidarity with a defeat of the spirit. But though Gloria Arkworth was as grey as slate within two weeks of her admission to hospital, her equally dramatic metamorphosis was pragmatic, and certainly voluntary. When she emerged from a fit of what the ward sister called the sulks, Gloria could have summoned the ever-loyal Samson of Topiary to her bedside for an application of the usual pink-blonde rinse. But Gloria didn't do this because one good look around told her that she would do best in her new context as an endearingly batty, sweet little old lady.

Gloria had been admitted suffering from malnutrition and severe headaches. The malnutrition diagnosis surprised no one who knew her normal diet, and the finding of Enda had confirmed that her recent interest in cooking had not been a new way of getting at Deborah. But the headaches, which soon abated, were probably the result of sleeping for weeks over several hundredweights of gelignite.

Due to a shortage of psycho-geriatric beds, Gloria had been placed in a general ward, among younger women with more painful but shorter-term problems such as bunions and torn knee cartilages. So Gloria, whose stay was to be mainly determined by the amount of weight she gained, was less uncomfortable than her neighbours and

166

correspondingly more cheerful. The student nurses who plumped up her pillows for her were soon joking that she was so good for morale that she ought to have been paid to be in hospital.

Gloria always had a knack for finding the soft touch. She sussed the orderlies worth winking at and the night nurse who most appreciated help with her knitting, and in no time at all she had a system worked out for the provision of little extras and the evasion of oppressive routines, such as the obligatory afternoon nap. But all this manoeuvring was quite harmless. Gloria's regular visitors were not asked to smuggle in jazz tapes, dill pickles or the banned cigarettes and booze. They brought talcum powder, frilly nighties, fruit, flowers and more knitting patterns. It was a fragrant old lady with a fluffy pink shawl around her frail shoulders, a regular invoker of the Name of the Good Lord, who chatted to them.

The returned Gordon Arkworth was absolutely delighted. It was good enough to be true. At last his mother had decided to grow old gracefully. Deborah could not be so uncomplicatedly happy about what she heard of the new Gloria, but she did not risk visiting her in person for fear of causing a relapse. Instead her good will was indicated by the loaves of bowel-busting fig bread she entrusted Frank with on his visits to the hospital. (The recipe was to be included in the practical back section of the book Deborah was writing with Karen Zucker.) Deborah was wary of Gloria's new image. She suspected that her mother-in-law was, literally, pulling the wool over her medical supervisors' eyes so as to qualify for an early discharge and a return to Chapel Grove before Gordon and Deborah had come to a proper rationalization of what remained of their relationship.

Because of Gloria's appropriate new enthusiasm for her 'grandson', Cora went in to see her almost every day. She felt as ambiguous as Deborah did about the change, though for different reasons. Cora had grown very fond of the old Gloria with her lipsticked teeth, her scarlet talons and her foul tongue and so she felt uncomfortable before this rocking-chair granny amidst her vases of cloying freesias. She found it hard to disguise her alienation and embarrassment, and as she sat one afternoon by Gloria's bedside, this may have been obvious. Gloria dipped into her stock of granny comments and fished out, 'You look a bit peaky today Cora dear, have you been taking your tonic?'

Cora mumbled something inconclusive back and desultorily fingered the box of chocolates brought in by Gordon on the previous afternoon. After having been measured for his latest woolly cape, Orlando had fallen asleep in the buggy, which was drawn up alongside the bed. Visitor and patient engaged in a further spate of half-hearted chat until a passing nurse was lassooed by Gloria with a flutter of frail hands.

'Sister,' Gloria whispered, though this nurse was no sister in either sense. (Cora was immediately reminded of Patrick's suggestion that it was always prudent to address all policemen as 'Officer, Sir'.) 'Sister, my niece here would love to have a cigarette. Would it be all right if we went down to the garden for half an hour.'

'Oh now,' said the nurse, smiling indulgently at Cora, 'we can't have you polluting our ward can we?' But even as she tut-tutted she was pulling a warmer robe from Gloria's locker, and telling Cora how to get to the courtyard garden by lift.

The 'garden' consisted of a dark yard in which some tubbed plants and a few wooden benches had been placed. No other patients were there, for the official visiting hour was now over and it was time for the afternoon sleep. Cora reckoned that Gloria had entered into some collusion with the nursing staff over her evasion of that afternoon curfew until she saw her, with something near her old cunning look, reaching into that patent leather handbag and pulling out a squashed filterless cigarette.

Between drags she said, 'If anyone comes down noseyparkering, I'll hand this over to you.' But the cigarette was not as delightful as anticipated and Gloria grimaced after she'd got halfway through it. 'Ugh,' she said looking at it disdainfully, 'stale as anything.'

'Shall I get you some more?' Cora's offer was made on sudden impulse, for this scenario, however bad for Gloria's physical health, was infinitely preferable to sweet talk up in the ward.

Gloria carried on spluttering and then shook her head. 'Too much trouble, don't bother,' she wheezed, 'but I've got something for you.' She dug her cigarette into a nearby tub of earth and began to root again in her handbag, eventually producing a crumpled envelope addressed to Miss Cora Mangan.

'Keep forgetting about this. I promised him I'd give it to you.'

Cora placed the letter in the breast pocket of her shirt. She did not want to read it there and then because this was the first opportunity she'd had of talking to Gloria about the experience that had sent her to hospital.

As though she could read Cora's thoughts, Gloria asked suddenly, 'What happened to him?'

'Enda?' Cora wanted to be sure that the old Gloria was really all there.

'They haven't told me anything, the bastards, and I have to keep my barmy act going just to get them to leave me alone.'

'I think,' Cora was still hesitant because she was afraid her news might be so upsetting as to undermine the possibility of future real conversations, 'I think they did get in touch with his family. I'm not sure, but one of them, one of his daughters, went to the post mortem.'

'Poor soul,' Gloria's eyes were wet and Cora handed her one of Orlando's wipes.

'He didn't know what to do with himself, or that stuff. He'd had it in his flat for months and months, but they

169

seemed to have forgotten all about it, and then the police started sniffing about.'

'So you said you'd mind it for him in your place?'

'It was the least I could do. He didn't charge much for all that work he did, and he was the kindest man that ever stood in shoe leather. It wasn't my cooking that killed him was it?'

'No,' Cora almost laughed, 'I'm sure you did just what he liked, but the trouble was, maybe he shouldn't have been eating like that. He had a bad heart you know.'

'No,' Gloria lit herself another squashed cigarette, 'he had a very good heart. He was a regular sweetheart.'

Cora said nothing more and then Orlando began to wriggle in his buggy. She fished in her own bag for a piece of carrot to give him and told Gloria she had to be going. On their way back to the ward Gloria gobbbled pellets of strong-smelling chewing gum and she winked at Cora as she climbed into her bed. 'You're a good girl and I won't forget you.' Until that day Gloria's now frequent references to her own death had disturbed Cora, but this one didn't, and for the first time since she'd started visiting her, she was genuinely sorry to leave the hospital.

After his supper that evening Orlando gave conclusive evidence of his dislike of scrambled free-range eggs by vomiting all over Cora's left shoulder. She wiped him down, gave him a drink and stripped herself to the waist. Next morning, when she was pulling her shirt out of the washing machine, she found the letter Gloria had given her. Although the paper was wet and the handwriting fuzzy, it was still perfectly legible:

Dear Miss Mangan
I have now been in touch with Mrs Betty Riordan and have confirmed that, through your good offices, she received the gratuity owing to her on the death of her husband on active service. I do hope this little matter has not caused you and your brother undue concern.

170

Beir bua agus beannacht
Enda Gallagher

That was how Cora found out that she'd been an unwitting
courier to Raging Bull's widow. Enda must have sloped off
to Welwyn Garden City to tell Mrs Riordan that the
helpful stranger's abandoned parcel was really her manna
from the movement. By leaving one of her parcels under-
neath Mrs Riordan's baby buggy, Cora had accidentally
cut out the middleman for the distribution of the contingency fund. But that was all to the good, fair enough as
Patrick said, for hadn't Cora proved that she was in no
need of a share in it? Patrick himself benefited directly
from Enda's mission because he had repossessed his
father's gold watch, which must have been wrapped up
with the money and which Enda had probably hoped to
return to him in the Crown. As for the Luger, Cora could
only think that it had indeed been the boat baby's legacy,
not that she or Patrick had any intention of trekking to
Welwyn Garden City to deliver it to him.

Although Gloria had gained weight and pleased her doctors enough to have been allowed out for occasional day
trips with the Fernwood Over-Sixties Club, she had under-
gone something of a moral relapse since Cora's last visit.
The ward sister told Gordon that she had been caught
smoking in bed in the middle of the night, and he quizzed
Cora, Patrick and Vivien in turn about how she might have
acquired the cigarettes.
   'Who could have been so irresponsible?'
   'I've no idea, but she has had a lot of her old friends in to
see her lately, and Leander's Mum's in the same ward for
her bunions.' Cora volunteered this information as in-
nocently as she could.
   'Leander?'
   'A young man she knows. His mother knits things for
Nativities.'

Gordon moaned and covered his California-burnished face with his hands. It was difficult to be his mother's keeper when she had such an unending supply of willing co-conspirators, and the ward sister terrified him. After lengthy discussions with Deborah, he had booked his mother into a private home in Kent, where her upkeep would be paid for by the proceeds from the sale of her part of the Chapel Grove house to Frank Watson. Gordon was quite prepared to leave Gloria in Kent while he himself returned to America, and Frank and Cora, among many others, had said that they would visit her regularly.

But Gloria would have none of this plan. She didn't want to go to some 'bleeding cattery' in the country. She liked it where she was, thank you very much. Besides which, one of the hospital chaplains (of which particular brand Gordon did not know) had informed Gloria of an alternative scheme that was, literally, right up her street. This was the Fernwood Senior Citizens' Centre, a block of ground-level maisonettes recently refurbished with the help of an injection of public funds, although there was no evidence that anyone over seventy had been involved with the riot. Gloria had good reason to believe that her neighbours there, some of whom she had met as fellow patients, would not object to her music or to the hours that she kept. Moreover, her doctor was nearby and her crisis had plugged her into a many-faced regiment of social workers and 'fellow' Christians.

So the wretched Gordon had returned from the hospital on his shield. But Deborah was kind to him. She said she was satisfied with a Gloria who would not be under her feet and a general consolation was derived from the apparent end of Mrs Arkworth's career as a petty criminal.

CHAPTER EIGHTEEN

As requested by her newly delivered sister, Vivien had taken Orlando's afterbirth out into the back garden and dug it in around the rose bushes. Vivien suspected that next door's cat had consumed the magnificently meaty, less than thoroughly buried placenta as soon as she'd crept back indoors for her ration of champagne. Nevertheless, Deborah took a great personal delight in the prolificity of the roses during the following summer. These blessed roses, which now benefited from a compost heap fuelled by Orlando's nappies, were still blooming in the week before his first birthday, and so Deborah decided to celebrate with a garden party. This idea was as practical as it seemed appropriate because Gloria's cleaned-up kitchenette was available as a catering centre with direct access to the fragrant garden.

To all intents and purposes his 'christening', Orlando's party was set to be a big affair. Deborah's world consisted of her friends and her enemies and because there was no transitional status between these two categories she was determined not to lose any of the friends through a false economy in its scale. Leonie Baxter and her friend Marlene were invited, for example, because Leonie had been forgiven for the nanny article and, as a sufferer from Karen Zucker's bowel syndrome, she was committed to a favourable interest in Deborah's new mission.

Helping Deborah with the party preparations was one way for Cora to earn the wages still paid to her since Frank had taken over much of her former responsibility for Orlando's welfare. Frank the one-time watcher-man had earned his leisure from his authorship of a software program for political journalists. His computers were now installed in the basement at Chapel Grove and he had taught Cora how to use a word processor. Ever gallant, he chose to see Cora as an ally rather than an obstacle to his rehabilitation. Her part in uniting him with Orlando was, he insisted, like that of Moses' big sister, who had fetched Miriam for the pharoah's daugher. Cora found the Moses joke tedious and she could not help cringing when Frank waxed sentimental about her Uncle Willy, but she could only be grateful for his benign interest in her future. Immediately, that looked respectable enough. Her examination results had given her a place at a London polytechnic, which she hoped to accept without worry on the basis of free accommodation at Chapel Grove in return for babysitting and part-time work with Deborah's mail-order firm.

Cora's new status in the revised household also derived from Patrick's installation in Vivien's flat, for the emergency public funding that had refurbished the Fernwood Senior Citizens' complex had also facilitated a sudden acceleration of plans for the demolition of Rochdale Gardens. Still, no 'announcement' was forthcoming from the flatmates, although Patrick had visited a dentist and Vivien emphatically treated Cora as a sister-in-common-law. She bleached Cora's ever-shorter hair and supervised her wardrobe so that she no longer looked as if she were trying to blend into the background.

Gloria had settled into her maisonette on the Fernwood prairie. The big front window was open and two small boys were collecting snails in the yard when Patrick came by to see about some shelves for the jazz albums that had migrated with their owner from Chapel Grove. Gloria heard him talking with the snail-hunters and from inside

174

her new parlour she called out as gaily as the pig in the brick house, 'Come right in, just push the door through.' So Patrick edged his way into the hallway and alongside a gallery of religious posters, pausing for a moment before an invitation from the World Vision of Christ to a 'deliverance rally' on the forthcoming weekend.

'I'm just here to measure up your music corner,' he shouted in her direction, 'but you didn't warn me to bring me garlic.' Only the hum of a vacuum cleaner answered his sarcasm. Gloria switched the machine off as he entered the room.

'Well,' he started up again, 'this is all coming along very nicely, and I see that you've covered yourself with the local Jesus companies.'

Gloria sniffed with dignity. Then she pointedly glanced down at the pale grey carpet made muddy by her visitor's sneakers, and turned the vacuum cleaner on again. Patrick took the hint. With his back to her, he set to work with his measure. Only when he'd listed the proposed music corner's dimensions did she stop cleaning a room that would have spread a smile of gratification over the face of the ward sister at St Phillip's Hospital. She went off into her kitchen, politely but firmly out of bounds to visitors, and emerged bearing a tray of tea and biscuits. With one eye on the miraculous medal pinned to his hostess's fluffy breast, Patrick renewed his enquiries.

'Does Father Mahon think you might take an option on his lot then?'

'Father Mahon is a lovely boy, and he knew my Enda.'

'Did he now?' Patrick took a sip from his china cup, which had received the lips of every cleric in the vicinity within the previous fortnight, and grimaced. No sugar. Somewhat ungraciously, Gloria fetched him some but then, rather than sit down with him, she began to dart around the room with a pink feather duster.

'Come on now Gloria. I mean it's okay for some old dears, but you've never needed people to keep you com-

175

pany because they think it's their Christian duty.'

'It's a comfort. I like the music and the Pope's dead right isn't he, about the pill and that.'

'Sure.' More mud fell from Patrick's sneakers as he stretched back on the sofa. 'And poverty's bad, peace's good, that there Pope sure hits the nail. . . .'

The tête-à-tête was violently interrupted by the thud of a ball against the front door. Gloria stood erect and with something of her old ferocity glinting in her eyes she scampered off to remonstrate loudly with the 'filthy little snivellers' who had almost certainly taken cover within earshot. Patrick laughed and his teacup rattled in its saucer. The returned Gloria smiled grimly and signalled some détente by producing an ashtray and a bottle of sherry from her lustrous cocktail cabinet. (This magnificently veneered item was one of the few possessions she'd bothered to take to her new premises.)

'Cheers!' Patrick raised his glass. 'Sure we're all settling down, getting on,' he pointed at the greying crown of his head, 'getting more mature.'

'Is that what you think you're about with that Salome sample?'

'That's not very Christian Gloria. I thought you might wish us a happy future or something banal like that.'

Gloria snorted and downed her overly modest glass of sherry without meeting Patrick's toast. He shot a look at the king-sized Bible atop the cocktail cabinet. 'Look, I won't give you any romantic blather about it, I know you wouldn't wear it and I'm not asking you to. But me and Viv, we've got something going for us right now, what you might call a coincidence of interests.'

'Cora tells me you're even sharing an accountant these days.'

'Yep. My sister's a very reliable informant.'

'Well don't come to me with your miseries.' And with that benediction Gloria unscrewed the cap of her sherry bottle once more and chinked her glass against Patrick's with a grudging 'Amen'.

The grass at the back of Chapel Grove had been cut and trestle tables set up. Patrick had built the barbecue upon which Deborah was permitting various meats to be cooked, since this was an acceptably anthropological form of carnivorism. Ahmed's wife Amrit had supplied Bengali vegetarian delicacies and the woman who made birth cakes for Nativities had made Orlando's birthday cake. (The same lady also catered for those clients who wished to eat suitably cooked and served afterbirths.) But the afternoon of the party was a rather precariously overcast one.

Cora weaved in and out of the guests in a spiral motion with a bottle of wine in each of her hands and told Gloria that she was allowed to smoke outdoors. Vivien dragged the inevitable representatives of her emotional past up to be introduced to Patrick as he tended the fire, and Karen Zucker, whom Deborah had designated as 'cosmic other-person', crooned over her one-year-old godson. But the uncertain weather meant that the real business of the day, Frank Watson's ratification as Orlando's father, had to be done quickly. Of all of the party's incidental significances, including Cora's coming of age and Gloria's departure, this was the most important, and Deborah was resolved to achieve it in no uncertain fashion. Accordingly, Gordon's presence had been ordered so as to make it clear that there was no contest, and no acrimony, over the paternal title.

At four o'clock Vivien and Karen Zucker mobilized the guests around the cake table and Deborah, with Frank holding Orlando by her side, shushed them all with a wave of a great cake knife.

'The Anglo-Saxons,' her speech began, to mock groans from the crowd, 'whom I cannot number among my own forebears, although my son can,' at this there was a meaningful glance at Frank, 'apparently believed that a child could be exposed if he, or more usually she, had not yet been formally named. So by this custom Frank and I should have been at liberty to place Orlando on the doorstep until this day because he has not yet been so named. Today, on his first birthday,' Deborah checked her watch, 'we are making good that omission. . . .'

At this point, in response to a discreet signal from Frank, Vivien raised her glass and cut Deborah's speech short with a raucous 'Happy Birthday!' Orlando gurgled obligingly and Frank put some cake icing in his mouth, and then everyone began to sing in spontaneous solidarity against what would almost certainly have been a lengthy sermon from Deborah. The threatened rain held off until most of the cake had been consumed and Patrick's fire was low. The surprisingly cheerful lute-playing couvade candidate helped Cora to carry leftover perishables indoors and even invited her to a concert, while Karen Zucker quizzed Amrit about Bengali attitudes towards the digestive tract.

Orlando's first year as a social being had been Cora's first as an adult, the year when she realized that people never grow up. All around her were the betrayals and contradictions that proved any belief in maturity to be childish: the Deborah who was quite happy, despite all of her rhetoric, to construct something very like the odious nuclear family; the Vivien who was prepared to be monogamous with a man who had said he'd never settle down; even the Gloria who ironed her underwear. But more of the same was to come.

The tea-chests destined for Frank and Deborah's weekend cottage in Wiltshire were blocking up the hallway at Chapel Grove when Cora answered the telephone to her Uncle Willy.

'Willy,' she yelled into the phone, sure that this was a long-distance call and that some dire calamity had compelled her uncle to use an instrument he had an unreasonable fear of.

'Didn't you hear me right? It's your Uncle Willy,' he repeated.

'Yes. What's wrong?'

'Nothing's wrong. I'm grand, we're grand.' Though she had not spoken with him since she and Patrick had rung him up on Christmas Day, Cora recognized a familiar testiness in her uncle's voice, and she quickly offered him the phone number of Vivien's flat. Later that day Patrick and Vivien called round to collect Cora and bring her into the West End, where her uncle was on honeymoon with his thirty-five-year-old bride, one Sadie-Dian Kelly, châtelaine of Rathbwee's hippy household.

Patrick thought it was very funny. 'The old codger's found someone to keep his bed warm in his old age,' was his comment, and he and Vivien were giving serious consideration to Willy's retirement plan. He wished to move into the purged hippy house with his bride and to leave the running of the bar to his nephew and, by her own implication, Vivien. Cora felt funny about it all, which wasn't the same thing as thinking it was very funny. She was her old silent self as pleasantries were exchanged in the lounge of the seedy Bloomsbury hotel where Willy and Sadie were staying.

In a lace-up leather bodice, Vivien was already playing the part of the publican's bait and Patrick asked Sadie about the viability of a bookshop-pub in Rathbwee. But no one shrivelled when Sadie pointed out the high overheads attendant upon such an enterprise, and she knew all about that since the loss of those exotic, yoghurt-yielding goats. Vivien even laughed at her warnings and clutched the wrist upon which Patrick Mangan Senior's gold watch gleamed.

Sadie bore herself with all of the acned dignity Cora remembered from her days as the harassed, receiptwielding manager of the hippy household's budget, and in clogs and a long paisley skirt she had made no concessions to London. As for Willy, in the Aran sweater his wife had knitted for him and rather baggy denim jeans, he looked the goatish bit all right. But Cora herself provoked the most comments for a certain inconsistency.

'Aren't you the real little Bobby Dazzler now?' said Willy, jabbing at her with his pipe, 'sure I wouldn't have recognized you. And there isn't a pick on you. Has she been eating anything at all?' He turned to Patrick, who said that as far as he knew Cora still had a good appetite. Cora nursed the shandy bought for her before she'd had a chance to demand anything more sophisticated and winced.

'Sadie!' she said, making a direct appeal to her new aunt and making it clear that she had independent prior knowledge of her, 'have you ever heard from Steve?'

Sadie frowned as she sifted through her memories of the countless Steves who had summered in Rathbwee, and Patrick glanced up from the theatre programme he was studying with Willy and Vivien.

'Oh yeah,' Sadie thought she had located the relevant Steve, 'the guy who was so scared about the wart on his prick?'

'Yes,' said Cora, nodding knowledgeably and pushing an ashtray in her uncle's direction, 'I just wondered if you'd ever heard from him.'

'Naw. He never paid what he owed. I guess he just went back to the States for a check-up.'

While Cora agreed with Patrick's suggestion for a night out on the town she could not help dwelling on this new twist to the course of her own little history. Scholars delight in speculating about the impact of the chance and the trivial on history: the attack of gout that dissuaded the all-conquering Ottoman Beyazid from marching into Central Europe, the fever caught on a duck-shoot that disabled Trotsky at a crucial time in his quarrel with Zinoviev, Kamenev and Stalin. In her gentle heart Cora Mangan pondered how she'd found herself in the hairy arms of Raging Bull Riordan and on the boat to England all because of a worrying wart on a shy man's penis.